THE
CONSEQUENCE
GIRL

**Also from
Alastair Chisholm**

For Younger Readers:

Dragon Storm: Tomas and Ironskin
Dragon Storm: Cara and Silverthief
Dragon Storm: Ellis and Pathseeker
Dragon Storm: Mira and Flameteller

THE CONSEQUENCE GIRL

ALASTAIR CHISHOLM

nosy
crow

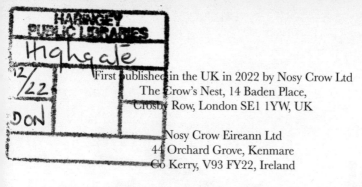
First published in the UK in 2022 by Nosy Crow Ltd
The Crow's Nest, 14 Baden Place,
Crosby Row, London SE1 1YW, UK

Nosy Crow Eireann Ltd
44 Orchard Grove, Kenmare
Co Kerry, V93 FY22, Ireland

Nosy Crow and associated logos are trademarks and/or registered
trademarks of Nosy Crow Ltd

Text © Alastair Chisholm, 2022
Cover artwork © Dan Mumford 2022

The right of Alastair Chisholm to be identified as the author of
this work has been asserted.

ISBN: 9781839941207

Printed and bound in Great Britain by Clays Ltd, Elcograf S.p.A.
Typeset by Tiger Media

Papers used by Nosy Crow are made from wood grown in
sustainable forests.

MIX
Paper from
responsible sources
FSC
www.fsc.org   FSC® C018072

1 3 5 7 9 10 8 6 4 2

nosycrow.com

For Mum and Dad, who showed me we can always make the world a little better.
A.C.

We have it in our power to begin the world over again.
Thomas Paine

Prologue

Whorley's day was going pretty well, until Lilith walked in.

He'd spent the morning in the markets of Sheen, under the vast steel crossbeams of the main chamber. He'd chatted, joked, tasted samples and slapped his large belly cheerfully before moving on. Nothing important, just seeing, and being seen. Whorley was a fixer – someone who could help with whatever you wanted, for a very reasonable price. So he made sure people remembered him, and were pleased to see him. It was easy, really; Whorley liked people, and he liked to help.

For a very reasonable price.

And then later he'd wandered back to the bar he owned, eaten a light lunch and read the report from his agents about a business venture that had taken place that morning. The results were everything he'd hoped. Yes, it had been a good day.

But that was Lilith for you. Lilith tended to happen to people who had been, up to that point, having a good day.

She strode in while he was finishing and sat down heavily in a chair across from him. The table rocked, and drops spilled from his glass.

"Whorley, you pig, you get greedier every day," she said without smiling. "How come you're not dead?"

Whorley sighed, but only on the inside. On the surface, he smiled as if Lilith was the person he'd hoped to see most in all the world. "Apple schnapps, my dear," he said amiably. "The apples are healthy."

He waved towards the bar, and Shaff, the barman – who had been lurking with one hand under the counter – relaxed and brought a bottle across. Whorley poured Lilith a glass.

"And you?" he asked. "Still a crazy troublemaker, are we? Cheers."

He raised his glass and examined her as he sipped.

Lilith was tall, almost two metres in her thick red-soled boots, with wide powerful shoulders. She wore a maroon leather jacket with plates of blast-proof steel sewn into it, and leather leggings. Whorley couldn't see it, but he knew she kept a small, vicious crossbow in a holster behind her

2

back. An old scar curved down the left side of her head, a gleaming pale line against her dark skin and short brown hair.

"You're looking well," he said lightly. (This was a lie. She was sitting stiffly, at an angle, and Whorley suspected her side was injured. And she looked tired.) "What can I do for you?"

Lilith didn't drink the schnapps. She gazed into the glass.

"Anything going on, Whorley?" she asked quietly.

Whorley spread his hands and grinned. "You know me, always busy. Why, are you looking for work?"

She shook her head. "No. Anything in Base? This morning?"

Whorley frowned. "You know I can't discuss my … *business operations*," he said. "My clients expect discretion."

Lilith looked out of one of the bar's small windows. It didn't point outside, of course – property on the outer shell of Sheen was far too expensive – but showed the inner balcony, and the people bustling past.

"There was a hit this morning," she said. "An item was taken. I want it back."

"You think I took it?"

Lilith shrugged. "There were several agents involved. They had equipment. They were careful. It had your

3

style." Her left foot was tapping against the table. Tap-tap-tap, like a nervous tic.

Whorley sighed.

"No," he said. "My people were in Sheen this morning. On a... Well, a mission. We don't need the details. But not Base."

He leaned back. "Whatever you lost, it wasn't me. Sorry."

She turned back from the window and stared at him for a long time. Then she nodded.

"I see."

Whorley frowned. "What was it – something of yours?"

"Something I was guarding." Her head dropped. She was exhausted, Whorley thought. He wondered how bad the injury to her side was. "For the Reverents."

"Oh, Lilith!" Whorley snorted. "I've told you not to work for religious types; they never pay!" He shook his head. "Come and work for me again. I'll give you a good rate. You and Anish too. I like him. You two still together?"

Lilith shrugged.

"Really," said Whorley, relaxing now. "Those people, they make you as crazy as them. Look at you. You get hit – all right, it happens – but then you barge in on me? Like you don't have enough problems? I've got three

4

guards watching this place right now. You could have been killed!"

He raised his glass. "Come on. It's just a job. Drink."

"Yes," she said. Her shoulders seemed to unknot, and she picked up the glass. "Yes."

"To the Lady Nostic and the Glories," he intoned, and drank.

Lilith was still looking at her glass. "Four," she said, at last.

"What?"

"You had four guards."

He didn't even see her hand move. Didn't see the thick-bottomed glass as it flew towards him, was only vaguely aware at first when it hit him right between his eyes with a *thunk*. He spun back over his chair and crashed to the ground, and before he could even cry out she was crouched over him, her small crossbow in one hand, ready to fire.

"You had *four* guards," she spat. "One at the entrance. Two on the balcony. One on deck eleven. You had four, now you have *none*, understand?"

Whorley made a sound like a thin, whistling wail. She knelt on his chest, crushing him.

"I want it back," she hissed. "No lies, no games, just you and me and this –" she waved the crossbow "– and I

5

want it back."

"Lilith … *please*," he gasped. "You're wrong, I swear. I wouldn't do that!" He thought one of his ribs had broken. He couldn't stop blinking. He could smell fermented apples and blood. "I love you guys! You and Anish, you're my—"

"Anish is *dead*!" she shouted. "He was killed this morning, in *your* raid!"

Whorley stared up at her in genuine horror. *Oh no*, he thought. *Oh, she's really going to kill me.*

Lilith glared at Shaff the barman, who was shuffling towards them and holding a club uncertainly.

"Put it down," she ordered. "Bring the item." Her tone was expressionless, but Whorley saw a pulse beating hard against her temple, and a thin trickle of blood at the bottom of her jacket. The wound in her side had opened.

Shaff hesitated. Lilith knelt harder, and Whorley felt a new shard of pain against his heart. Yes, one rib definitely broken. He waved feebly. "Go," he wheezed. "Go."

The barman hurried through to the back. Whorley closed his eyes. "You're crazy," he muttered. "This is crazy."

Lilith said nothing.

"They said it was a clean job," he whispered. "I thought it was clean. I didn't know about Anish—"

She shifted her knee against him and he groaned.

Shaff returned with a rectangular box half a metre wide and deep and a little longer, carrying it by a handle on the top. He put it down and stepped back. Lilith stood and peered inside.

The box was lined with fur. Inside, wrapped in a blanket, was a sleeping baby, with pale fawn skin and a short crop of straight black hair. One hand was outside the blanket, fingers curled.

Lilith picked up the box.

"What are you going to do with it?" gasped Whorley. She ignored him. "You know what it is? What they say about it? You can't give it back to the Reverents, Lilith!"

"I'm not giving it to them," she said.

"To Protection?" He coughed. "That's who *I'm* selling it to! You could just leave it with me. I can give you a cut—"

"Not Protection."

"But... But who, then?"

Lilith put the little crossbow back into its holster and walked towards the entrance with the box.

"Goodbye, Whorley."

Whorley stared in astonishment. Was she letting him *live*? What was going on? The pain in his ribs was vicious, but he tried to ignore it a little longer.

7

"Lilith, wait! Anish—"

She turned, her face dark with something he didn't want to know.

"I never meant…" He shrugged helplessly. "I'm sorry."

For a moment he thought she was going to shoot him right there. But eventually she sighed and checked her watch.

"Seven minutes," she said.

"Till what?"

"Till the people you thought you were selling to come to kill you."

"What? They're not coming to kill me." Whorley shook his head, more in confusion than denial. "I got it *for* them. It's just a deal."

Lilith shrugged. "That's not the deal they made."

She left with the package. He watched her go in a daze, and groaned as he sat up.

"You all right, boss?" asked Shaff.

Whorley found the strength to slap the barman about the head. "Of course not, you cretin." He closed his eyes. Lilith was wrong. He had a deal – just business, same as every other time. She had to be wrong.

"Boss?"

"Help me stand," he muttered. Shaff lifted him up, and Whorley tried not to scream as his ribs protested.

"I think…" he said, when he could speak again, "I think we should go out the back."

Lilith went down three levels and into a hidden recess. She discarded the box and used the blanket to fasten the baby girl to her back, wincing as she tied it tight. Then she climbed down a long access ladder to a hatch that led her out of Sheen, and on to the ground.

Seven minutes after she left, a team of Protection troops raided Whorley's bar with orders to retrieve a package and destroy everything and anyone else they found.

A few days later, a figure in a plain brown jacket and jeans limped through the tiny settlement of Recon, before following a faint track up into the mountains. One or two people in Recon watched her as she entered the settlement, but when they saw the expression on her face they turned away until she had passed, and if they noticed the sling on her back, they never mentioned it to anyone.

Thirteen Years Later

Cora

The light was turning as Cora reached the east side of the mountain, and there was already a hint of dusk. It was a cold light, and it leached the colour from the world, leaving the trees black and the ground white, and pinching her hands and face.

She followed the stream to a point where three faint rabbit tracks met, where she had set a snare the previous day. It lay undisturbed. *Blast*, she thought, but said nothing. She checked the loop and moved it further into the path of the tracks. Four traps and nothing so far. She'd hoped to stock up, but at this rate they'd be eating into their supplies. She stuffed her hands into her jacket and made her way along a snow-clad ridge to the last two spots.

The world was silent. Birds huddled quietly on their branches, small animals stayed in their burrows, and the cabin where Cora lived was the only one occupied for kilometres around. Most people preferred to stay in Recon, far below and on the other side of the hill. It was a hard climb to the ridge, through snow, and when she reached the top Cora stopped to catch her breath and looked down at the settlement.

She could see the Recon Tower, a hexagonal column with large windows, and smaller buildings huddled around its base as if for protection. The tower was built of the same almost indestructible material as everything else the Glories had left behind, and despite being ancient it shone newer and cleaner than its neighbours.

On one side of the tower, the loading bay was stacked high with tree trunks, ready for delivery to the cities of Sheen and Base. She could make out the faint outlines of more buildings, perhaps even a little wood smoke from their chimneys, but she was too far away to see any people. She watched for a while, and then turned and trudged to the next snare.

Here at last was something; a small and rather scrawny rabbit with one leg caught in the loop. It lurched as she arrived, trying to escape, but then collapsed, exhausted. Cora looked around for a rock. Seleen could dispatch them with her bare hands, breaking their necks in one sharp tug, but Cora wasn't strong enough, and anyway, she found it too upsetting. The rock was brutal but quicker. Grimacing, she killed it quickly, unwound the sticky wire from its body, packed it into her bag and reset the trap. There was dinner, at least. She headed down to the last trap, but knew there was something wrong even before she reached it. There was no catch, but the ground was churned up – and the snare was gone.

"Blast!" This time she swore out loud, and two birds above her flapped away, cawing indignantly. Losing a rabbit was bad; losing wire was *really* bad. Seleen would be furious. The stake was still there, wedged firmly into the ground. What had happened? Was it another predator? A wolf? That would be worst of all.

The sun was slipping past the edge of the ridge now. Cora looked around cautiously. She was alone, of course. Seleen was back at the cabin. Cora hesitated. Then she sat on her haunches and made herself relax, gazing at the stake. The stake was here. The snare was gone. She closed her eyes, let her focus drift … and *looked*.

She saw the stake in her mind, surrounded by a weak shimmer like a heat haze. As she drifted closer, the shimmer became a faint blue trail, as if the stake was moving while sitting still. She followed the trail backwards in time.

In her mind, the stake trembled. It was a few hours ago, and something was pulling at it. What? The stake

14

was being dragged by its snare, which in turn was being pulled by a large rabbit, caught but furiously heaving away. The rabbit tugged and tugged, and suddenly the wire slipped off its stake, and the rabbit ran, dragging the snare behind.

The wire had slipped. The wire had slipped because…

She saw herself setting up the trap. Her hands were cold and sore, and her face was tired. Cora watched this other, earlier version of herself wind the wire into a loop, fasten it, attach it to the stake, wrap it once…

In her mind she heard an owl shriek, and the earlier Cora looked up, then finished wrapping the cable. But she was distracted and keen to get home, and she forgot to thread it through the hole in the stake.

There.

Cora opened her eyes again and waited until her focus came back. There was always a short feeling of disorientation after she *looked*, and a dull red throb behind her eyes. She groaned.

Not a wolf then, at least. But it was her fault; she hadn't fastened the snare properly, and now it was lost. Cora examined the stake. She could fix it, perhaps. It had happened less than a day ago. *I could fix it…*

She sighed. No. Seleen had a way of finding these things out. It wasn't worth it, not even for a snare.

* * *

Cora returned to their cabin. It sat squat under a wide camouflage net that spread across the hillside, woven with creeping ivy and fresh leafy branches. It was almost invisible, even up close, and she approached it from a different direction each time, automatically glancing around before entering.

Seleen was outside, under the net, working on the power unit. Cora always crept the last stretch, but had never been able to sneak up without being spotted. This time she was twelve metres away when Seleen, without lifting her head out of the unit, said, "You're back early."

Cora shrugged. "Most of them were empty. One catch."

Seleen grunted, still under the cover.

Cora said, "And we lost a snare as well."

Seleen stood up straight and studied her.

Seleen was tall, and looked strong enough to wrestle bears. She ran a hand through her silvered brown locs, revealing an old scar on the side of her head. When Cora was younger, Seleen used to tell her she'd got the scar fighting a giant robot, and Cora had believed her. These days she was sure it wasn't true, of course. Fairly sure.

"How?" Seleen asked.

"Pulled loose."

Seleen frowned. "By what? A wolf? Did you check for wolf tracks?"

"No, a rabbit. It was just—"

"A rabbit can't pull one of those snares." Seleen scanned the hillside, thinking. "If it's a wolf then it might try to raid."

"It was just a rabbit, OK?" said Cora irritably. "I didn't fasten the snare properly."

Seleen gave her a hard look. "Hmmm. You're sure?"

Shrug. "Yes."

"*Really* sure?"

"Yes!"

There was a pause. Then… "*How* are you sure, Cora?"

Cora started. *Blastblastblast!*

"Did you *look*?" asked Seleen.

Cora didn't answer, which was answer enough. Seleen slammed the power unit cover down with a clatter.

"What's the Rule?" she demanded. Cora stared at the ground. "Cora? What's the Rule?"

Cora muttered, "I Mustn't Look."

"You Mustn't Look. And why not?"

"Because It's Dangerous."

"Because it's *dangerous*. Because you can do more harm than you think."

"I don't see how!" Cora, thin and small, faced up to

17

her. "It's only looking. I didn't *change* anything! I could have fixed it so we didn't lose the snare—"

"No, you *couldn't*," snapped Seleen, "because that would have been really *stupid*." She was angry now. "You know how you could have *not* lost the snare?"

"Yes, by—"

"By fastening it properly! What have I told you? No do-overs in this life, understand? No second chances! When you mess up, there are *consequences*."

They squared up against each other, breathing hard and glaring, but Cora blinked first. As she always did.

"*Fine*," she muttered. She stomped into the house, slammed the cabin door so hard that the frame creaked, and threw the rabbit corpse on to the table.

That evening they ate in silence. Cora had skinned and cooked the rabbit in a thin stew that was mostly small, hard potatoes and kale, but Seleen didn't comment. She chewed mechanically and ignored the girl seething at the other end of the table.

Finally she wiped the plate with a piece of bread. "I fixed the power unit," she said.

Cora grunted.

"So no more heating failures."

Grunt.

"But we'll need another power cell soon, before the heavy snows set in. And more wire, of course."

Cora said nothing, and Seleen sighed and stood up, and heated some water in a pan. Cora took the food scraps outside.

It was almost pitch dark, and she was careful to close the inner door before opening the outer one, to stop the light from showing. She felt ice on the wind as she walked to the roost and tipped the scraps into the chickens' trough, listening to their sleepy clucks. She trudged back in blackness; she knew every stone and slope around the cabin so well she didn't need to see.

When she re-entered, Seleen was sitting at the table, with two cups in front of her. Steam rose from them, and Cora realised she could smell ... *chocolate*.

Seleen gave a twisted, slightly awkward smile.

"Peace offering," she said.

Cora glared at the cups, trying to keep a stern face, but their scent wafted over her like a blanket and she shook her head and smiled.

"Hmmph," she managed, and sat. They sipped at the chocolate. It was delicious, and a luxury; they were nearly out. This might even be the last of it. Seleen read her thoughts and nodded.

"Jeb Harrow will be coming past tomorrow, with

supplies," she said.

"We could use some pepper too," said Cora.

Seleen shrugged. "I'll see what he has."

They sat in silence, and then Cora got up and washed the pots and pans, and Seleen went to check the fences.

That evening, Cora lay awake, listening to Seleen snoring softly from the other bunk, and the occasional sound of night birds from outside. She thought of the big rabbit pulling the snare loose. Wire was scarce, but something inside her was glad it had escaped. She imagined it, tugging desperately, apparently hopeless, round and round in circles, and then – freedom!

She slept, and dreamed of its adventures on the snowy hillside, running free with the snare wire trailing behind.

Alone

The next morning, Cora was fixing a new coil for the oven when Seleen appeared at the doorway.

"Jeb's heading across," she said. Cora nodded. Seleen walked down the hill from the cabin, and Cora stopped her work and watched from the front window. Jeb was standing in the snow-covered meadow below them, where Seleen always met him. He said something – Cora heard his cheery voice in tiny snippets, too faint to make out – and Seleen nodded and replied.

Jeb was ancient; fifty, maybe more, even. He'd lived on the hillside his whole life, and his clothes were worn and reworked like Seleen's and Cora's, and patched with wolf pelt. He kept his grey hair in a ponytail, but his beard was short and patchy, and his face was red with sunburn. He smelled pretty ripe; sometimes Cora could recognise his scent all the way from the cabin.

She never spoke to him, but stayed inside whenever he came round. And Jeb never looked up towards her. This close, he might have been able to see the cabin through the camouflage, but he always acted as if there was nothing – as if Seleen had appeared out of thin air to trade. The mountain was a place for people who didn't want to be disturbed, and Jeb understood that. He kept to himself and only went into Recon for supplies. When he did, he usually brought back some to sell to Seleen.

Cora wondered what Recon was like. Seleen called it a dirt town. She said that meant it was small, but Cora knew there must be dozens of people living in all those houses. Perhaps even a hundred. She tried to imagine a hundred people...

Something wasn't right, she realised. Jeb had handed over some items, but he was shrugging. Eventually he hitched his pack back over his shoulder, waved and headed off, and Seleen returned, looking distracted. She tipped a few supplies on to the table.

"No chocolate," she said. "There'll be more in a couple of days."

Cora groaned. Seleen nodded. "No power cells either."

This was more serious. The cells provided all their power for the cabin: heat, light, tools. They were Glory technology, old and irreplaceable. "How come?"

"Jeb says they're running low; they've started rationing them. I have to go down and get one myself." Seleen looked out of the window. "It's no big deal."

It seemed to Cora like it was a big deal. Seleen was bothered and trying not to show it. It wasn't the journey to Recon; Seleen went down every few months for things Jeb couldn't bring up. But she didn't like change, Cora knew. New things made her twitchy.

"Well," said Cora. "The important thing is you'll be able to get some chocolate."

Seleen snorted. "Yeah." She squared her shoulders and turned back, smiling.

But Cora could tell she was worried.

"Remember to check the fences."

Cora sighed. "I always remember."

"And keep the nets repaired at all times. And don't let anyone see you come in or out."

"I won't."

Seleen heaved her backpack on.

"Pepper," said Cora. "And nails; we're almost out. Salt. And a microwave canister if they have one."

Seleen nodded, gazing down the valley towards the river that wound eventually to Recon. It was a nice morning and the sky was blue, but low, white clouds had gathered on the horizon.

"I'll be back Friday," she said, eyeing the clouds. "Maybe Saturday."

"I know."

"Power's good for a couple of weeks yet."

"I *know*."

Seleen nodded again. "Right. See you in a couple of days." She slipped out from under the camouflage netting and strode down the hill.

For a moment Cora felt an urge to follow her down, to the bottom of the valley at least. But she knew Seleen wouldn't like that. So she stood at the edge of the netting and watched until the woman disappeared between a tangle of trees. Until Cora was alone. She looked out across the hillside, and the snow-covered trees. Far off in the distance, a bird cawed.

Cora went back inside.

The day passed.

She checked the traps first. Seleen insisted she take a different route each day, so that they didn't build up trails between the snares. Cora liked to work out the distances in her head. Exactly two hundred metres from here to the cliff-edge trap. Then thirty-two metres to the next, or forty-one if she went by the large boulder…

24

She could often see the best, most efficient route to take, as if it was hanging in the air in front of her. She eliminated recent routes. She couldn't go from boulder to river today ... but she could go from boulder to cliff-edge, then to lee, then river. Fourteen hundred and seven metres. It was only a game, but it stopped her getting bored. And it stopped her thinking about being alone. Of course, she was always on her own when checking the traps, but somehow it felt different when Seleen was back at the cabin.

Three catches today and back for lunch. She made soup and drank it from a mug, sitting outside in the shadowy, forest-like light under the netting, and gazing at the view through a small opening. Seleen had probably reached the river by now. It would be another six hours to Recon.

Cora longed to be there with her. Seleen reckoned Recon was small, but it had the supply store, a magical place Cora had only heard of, full of food and equipment. And people. Other people. What would they be like? Like Jeb? Like Seleen? Like Cora, even?

She shook her head and went back inside to clear up. Then she checked the fences and nets, fed the chickens and collected their eggs, milked Juliet the goat, weeded the vegetable garden, finished repairing the oven, put some fresh bread on to bake, and tried not to think about the silence.

In the evening, she walked around the outside of the cabin, carefully closing every shutter. It was dark, just a shimmer of moonlight through cloudy skies. She saw the tiny dot of yellow light from Jeb's cabin, seven or more kilometres away, and watched it flicker.

After a while she went inside and switched her own lights on. She sat at the wooden table, hesitating. Then she retrieved a sheet of paper from under her bed, and a small charcoal stick, and, after a moment of thinking, drew a face.

It was a woman's face, with short black hair like Cora's, and a curving, smiling mouth. Cora frowned; she wasn't particularly good at drawing, and Seleen didn't encourage it. She didn't like it when Cora drew faces. But it was close enough.

She didn't know who it was. Cora had a good memory, but as far as she knew she had never seen this woman before. But occasionally – once or twice, perhaps – she'd awoken from a dream of a face, with shining eyes, black hair and soft brown skin. She gazed at the image, trying to remember. Nothing she could pin down. Nothing but a sense of warmth and … protection? Cora knew who she thought it was, although she would never say. She stared at the woman's mouth as if it was about to speak…

Then she shook her head, burned the paper to ashes, and went to bed.

Cora woke early and breakfasted on thick slices of new bread, and then she wrapped up and slipped out from under the nets.

Ridge first this time, then boulder, then lee. Not as efficient; fifteen hundred and thirty-one metres. The clouds pressed down against the hillside, subduing everything around her. Birds huddled silently on branches. From the ridge, she stared down the other side of the mountain, at Recon, trying to make out the buildings and any sign of people. Seleen was down there, somewhere.

She looked towards the far hills, where logging had carved a scar out of the landscape. It was too far to make out details, though sometimes she heard the echo of trees falling. Not today. Today was silence. She headed towards the traps on the far side, and then stopped.

Someone was calling.

It was a single call, faint. It could have been from far away, through the clear air, but she didn't think so. It felt near. Cora stayed absolutely still, keeping her breathing slow and quiet.

Nothing.

No sound, anywhere. A fall of old snow off a branch,

nothing else. Nothing—

"Help!"

There. Definitely close. Was it Jeb, fallen and hurt? It didn't sound like him. Cora's heart pounded. What should she do? She looked around, but nothing was moving. She bit her lip and waited again. Nothing. After a long time, she made her way towards where she thought the call had come from. She stepped carefully, keeping under cover of the trees, where a thick layer of fallen needles muffled the sounds of her boots. She stopped several times and waited, as still as a startled rabbit.

What would Seleen do, she wondered? She reached to her belt for the long, sharp hunting knife, and held it ready.

"Help!"

Closer now, but weaker too. Cora crept forward into a small clearing, and stopped.

At the far end of the clearing was a boy.

He was sitting leaning against a tree, with his eyes closed. He wore a thick coat and boots, and had a small bag next to him. His face was pale and screwed up in pain, and his mouth opened in rasping breaths.

A clump of snow fell from a branch next to Cora with a thud, and he opened his eyes and looked at her.

Cora gasped. He gasped too, and gazed at her as if he

thought she might be a dream. Then he croaked, "*Help.*"

She didn't move.

"My ankle," he said. "I think it's broken." His voice was clotted and thick with pain. After a moment, he lifted one arm. "Hello? Can you hear me?"

His hair was arranged into spikes, half-flattened. On one side, the hair was matted and tangled and thick. Thick with blood, Cora realised.

"Help," he said. "*Help me.*"

Cora stood at the edge of the clearing and stared at him until she could move.

Then she fled.

The Boy

Cora scrambled through the forest, panicking, her feet tripping against tree roots. Behind her, the boy called out again – "*Help me! Don't go!*" – but then started coughing. She fumbled through the camouflage nets, raced to the cabin, slammed and barred the door, and sat on her bed with her back against the wall and her hands around her knees, staring and panting.

He'd seen her!

She'd let him *see* her. The thing she absolutely couldn't do. And Seleen wasn't here; oh, why couldn't Seleen be here! What was Cora going to do?

Gradually her breathing slowed to normal, her heartbeat calmed and she tried to think. It was a boy. He was hurt, somehow. How? What was he doing here? *Why* was he here, why was he here *now* when Seleen wasn't, why—

She stopped. It was a boy, and he was hurt. What would Seleen do? She thought of the woman's face, grim and suspicious. Stay away, Seleen would say. Keep to ourselves.

Cora bit her lip. Nothing to do with us. Not our problem.

After a long time, she went to feed the animals and check the fence. Her eyes strayed towards the ridge, but she focused them back on her chores. The afternoon turned; thick clouds were forming. No new snow yet, but the air smelled of it. That evening, she lay in her bunk, in dim lamplight, and thought again: *Why is he here?*

She had to know. She *had* to.

She let her mind drift … and *looked*.

She started with the mat of bloodied hair on the boy's head. What had caused that? She let her attention float and settle on to the blood, then followed it back in time, to its cause … *there*. A ghostly image of his head scraping a rock to one side of the tree, the rock cutting skin.

What had caused that? She drifted further back. He'd hit the rock because he'd fallen from a tree. Why was he in the tree? Was he looking for someone? But she couldn't tell. She could only see cause and effect; she couldn't read minds. And she could see back only a day or so. Whatever had caused him to be on the hillside had happened earlier

31

than that. He was there, and that was that.

And he was hurt.

She tried to sleep, but every time her eyes closed she heard him calling – "*Help me!*" – until at last she fell into a thin half-doze that left her exhausted by dawn.

It was colder, and a bleached wind was slicing up through the trees, whistling and humming. She stared out of the window, down to the valley. Seleen would be days yet, at least. The clouds were thicker. A storm was coming.

Without admitting to herself what she was doing, she pulled on her coat and boots, left the cabin and walked up to the ridge.

The boy had dragged himself into the undergrowth for shelter and was curled up into a ball with his hands tucked into his armpits. He wasn't moving, and Cora thought for a moment he'd died overnight. She felt a mixture of guilt and relief at the idea, and then shame. But then he shuddered and gave a ragged breath.

She crept forward, hesitated, then tapped his cheek and pulled back. Nothing. He didn't move, or open his eyes, and his skin felt cold and clammy. She touched his face again, this time for longer. Still nothing.

So. Not dead, but not well. And unconscious.

Cora cut down three branches and laid them out into an "A". She needed rope. She checked the boy's pack and found spare clothes, some dried sausage, a water bottle. Then a few pieces of paper with drawings of the hillside from different angles, and a red velvet bag, full of strange white cubes.

The last item was a black case. It was made of Glory material, soft but strong, and inside was a device Cora didn't recognise, a thick black rectangle with two glass circles at each end. She stared at it. Glory technology – incredibly valuable, literally irreplaceable. How could this boy have it?

Cora shook her head and used the boy's boot laces to tie the branches. She studied him, biting her lip. Then, in one movement, she reached down, burrowed her hands under his body and heaved him on to the frame. He wasn't heavy, and Cora, though thin, was strong. He didn't move. She lifted one end and pulled him back down the hill.

It was hard work, and her makeshift sledge caught against trees and roots, but at last she made it under the camouflage nets and into the yard. She dragged him off the platform and inside the cabin, and opened the trapdoor to their cellar, the most secure place she could think of. With a huge effort she lowered him down by a loop of rope under his armpits. She tied his hands together and tethered him to a hook on the ceiling, long enough for him to lie down but not reach the trapdoor.

Would that hold him? Was he even unconscious? She wasn't sure, but she didn't think he was acting. He seemed genuinely ill, and she worried about the wound on his head. She fetched blankets and arranged a makeshift bed out of some old crates. The cellar was cold, close to bare earth, and she found a heater with a trickle of power left and switched it on.

She removed his coat, examining it curiously. It was made of real cloth, all in one colour, a warm dark red. He had a scarf and gloves but no hat, and his hair stood up in stiff, dyed-blue spikes. Under the coat was a jumper, and green trousers that stopped above his boots. Cora thought they looked impractical.

His face was somehow both sharp and soft, with fine cheekbones and smooth white skin, but pale almost to blue, and the blood on his head caked one side of his hair down into a clump. Cora fetched water and a cloth, and carefully cleaned the wound. To her relief, it was just a scrape, nothing worse. The ankle was puffed up and sore, but only sprained, not broken.

She bandaged his foot and covered him with a thick blanket. Finally she found an old bucket with a cover and placed it within reach. She climbed back up the ladder and closed and latched the trapdoor. Then she retreated to her bed, laid her knife beside her and sat watching, and wondering what to do next.

"Hello? Is anyone there? Hello?"

Cora snapped awake and grabbed her knife. Stupid. *Stupid* girl. The warm cabin, the lack of sleep the previous evening… *Seleen wouldn't have fallen asleep*, she thought.

"Hello?"

She peered down into the cellar through a gap in the floorboards. He was there, standing as far forward as the rope would allow, looking up.

"Hello? Is someone there?"

Cora closed her eyes for a moment and sighed. No point delaying.

"Move away!" she shouted.

The boy started. "Hello?"

"Move back. Hold your hands up."

He made a shuffling hop backwards and raised his hands. He was still tied. Cora unlatched the trapdoor, drew a breath and swung it open. He tried to take another step back but stumbled as the weight shifted to his right ankle, and collapsed on to the bedding.

"Ow!" he yelped.

"It's not broken," said Cora. "It's just sprained."

"Feels broken," he muttered.

Cora examined the boy from the top of the ladder. He was still pale.

"Are you thirsty?" she asked.

He looked up at her again and nodded.

Cora fetched a bucket of water from the keg and climbed down with it. She placed it within his reach, holding her knife ready. The boy watched her, but when a few drops splashed on to the ground he stared at them instead and licked his lips. Cora stepped back and he slithered forward on his knees, lifted the bucket, and drank, and drank.

"Not too fast," she warned.

He coughed, closed his eyes in relief and nodded. He took another, slower, sip and then put the bucket down and looked at her, and then at the rope on his wrists.

"Where am I?" he asked.

Cora didn't answer that. Instead she said, "Your head was hurt, but it's not serious. It will take a day or two for your ankle to recover."

The boy tried to move his foot and winced, and nodded. "Why am I tied up?"

He sounded worried, but not afraid. Cora thought he wasn't altogether awake. Again, she didn't answer his

36

question. "Are you hungry?"

"I'm Kai," he said. "What's your name?"

Cora shook her head. "You shouldn't be here," she said. "You shouldn't be anywhere *near* here. You get better and you go, understand? Before—" She stopped. *Before Seleen gets back*, she had been going to say.

"Yes," he said. Still, he didn't seem afraid.

"What?"

"Yes, I'm hungry. Starving, actually." He frowned. "I saw you, didn't I? In the woods."

"What were you doing there?"

He shrugged. "Fell out of a tree. Thought I was going to die. You saved my life." He smiled, as if he wasn't tied up, as if she wasn't holding a knife. "Thanks for coming back."

Cora chewed her lip. "I'll get you something to eat," she said. "Don't move."

He laughed as if she'd made a joke. She climbed back up and bustled about the stove, heating milk for porridge. She felt him watching her from below.

"You live here alone?" he called. Cora said nothing. "It's nice."

She brought the porridge down.

"Move back," she said, and he obediently shuffled towards his bed. She put the bowl down and stepped away, letting him come forward. He leaned over it and breathed in, and then made a strange gesture, tapping his forehead with a small bow. He lifted the spoon and tasted. Then he took another spoonful, and another, as fast as he could. When he was finished, he sighed and yawned.

"You should rest," said Cora.

He nodded and crawled back to the bed, and seemed to fall asleep in seconds. She watched him. His breaths were steady and relaxed.

Outside, Juliet the goat bleated, wanting to be fed and milked. Cora climbed up and shut the trapdoor, then hesitated. She opened and closed the front door, loudly. The boy didn't move. She waited a full minute, peering through the floorboards, but he didn't open his eyes. She opened the door again and left, closing it quietly this time, and sorted the animals.

Juliet was cross with her, butting her in agitation. Half the milk slopped out of the bucket. The chickens huddled together nervously. It was the weather, Cora thought. Grey layers were forming in the sky above. The wind had died, except for random sudden tufts, like danger signals whipping across the hillside. It was too early in the year for a big storm, but one was coming anyway.

Cora made sure the chickens had food and water, dragged Juliet into her shed and closed it, and returned to the cabin.

The boy was awake when she went back down. Cora found herself reaching for her knife, but resisted. She tried to think how Seleen would act, and strode towards him as if she wasn't nervous.

"How are you feeling?" she asked gruffly.

"Better," he said. "Thank you. But…" He seemed embarrassed. "I kind of need to, um…"

Cora nodded. "There's a bucket there," she said, pointing. "And sawdust there. I'll bring you water to wash with."

"Thanks."

She climbed back up and closed the trapdoor. She couldn't keep him like this, it was mad. What would Seleen say? What would happen when he was better? But what else could she have done?

She busied herself by hammering thick slats of wood around the trapdoor to make a proper lock. When she thought he'd had long enough, she brought him down a bowl of water. He was sitting back on the bed.

"What's going on?" he asked, holding his tied hands up. "Why this?"

Cora shook her head. "You get better, you go. We— I don't like strangers."

"I'm not a threat, I promise. My name's Kai."

"You said. Get better, go."

He nodded. "OK. What's your name?"

"No."

The boy laughed. "I have to call you something! Come on, just a name."

Cora shook her head again. "How's your ankle?"

He tested it. "Swollen. I can't stand on it."

"I've got some liniment to ease the swelling." She looked around. "Do you need anything else?"

He gazed at her. His eyes were green and soft.

"No," he said, and she nodded and headed back up the ladder.

"Only your name," he called.

She paused. "Why were you up that tree?"

"I'll tell you if you tell me your name," he said, grinning.

Cora scowled, and he laughed behind her as she locked the trapdoor. Just a day or two, she thought. Then he'd be fit enough to leave. He could be gone before Seleen returned; she wouldn't even have to know.

The cabin was dark, though it wasn't evening yet, and silent – the wind had dropped to nothing. Cora looked outside.

Snow was falling.

It was thick, steady, piling up on the windows and the

frozen ground. Very thick – she could see less than a metre or two beyond the window. And she could feel it too, in her skin; this would continue for the rest of the day, and all night, and perhaps the next day too. The pass to Recon would be blocked.

Seleen wasn't coming back any time soon. And the boy wasn't leaving either.

Snowbound

The cabin was ready for snow, weatherproof and snug. The larder was stocked, the animals were safe and there was still power. They just had to wait it out. But Cora was distracted. She checked and rechecked their supplies, watched the gauge on the power cell, tapping it for no reason. She tried to prepare a stew but burned the onions, spilled the oil, almost cut herself. She cursed.

"Everything all right?" came a call from the cellar.

She tried to focus. When the stew was ready she brought down a tray, and Kai obediently lifted his hands to show them still tied.

"You joining me?" he asked.

Cora shook her head, then realised she'd loaded two bowls on to the tray without thinking.

"I, ah, guess," she muttered, and found a small stool to sit on. The boy sniffed at his bowl, tapped his forehead

42

and tasted. It was awful, Cora knew; the onions and meat had burned and stuck to the pot, and the vegetables were mushy and tasteless.

"Delicious!"

"It's terrible," she said.

He shrugged. "Tastes good to me. I was on rations and rainwater for a week, and that was before I fell." He ate. "I like rabbit. Can't catch them though."

"We use— I use snares," she said.

He nodded. "Did you know they're not really rabbits?"

"What?"

"This—" He tapped the bowl. "It's not rabbit."

Cora frowned. "Of course it is."

"Nope. That's what the Glories *called* them. But it was a different animal back where they came from. They just called them rabbits because they looked a bit the same."

Cora peered at him suspiciously. "Really?"

"Yes!" He shrugged. "According to someone I know, anyway. He says the Glories named lots of animals after ones from their world."

Cora shook her head. Seleen didn't talk about the Glories much.

"You lived here long?" asked Kai. Cora didn't answer, and he smiled. "You don't say much, do you?"

She stood. "I'm going back up."

He raised his hands. "Sorry! Sorry. Please – sit, please."

She hesitated, but sat again.

"I'm from Base," he said. "You ever been there?"

"No." Base was a city, she knew; the capital city. Seleen had said it was the biggest in Colony, though Cora had struggled to understand. Hundreds of houses, Seleen had said. *Thousands*.

"You should go," said Kai. "I love it there. I like crowds." He shrugged. "I don't know if I could live here by myself, all alone…" His eyes flicked to her face, but she kept her expression blank.

"Are you finished?" she asked.

He sighed, and nodded. "I guess so. Look, tell me *something*. Anything. Where am I, even?"

"Why were you up that tree?" asked Cora.

Kai laughed. "I told you, if you want to know that, you'll have to tell me your name."

She took the tray and left.

"Goodnight," he called.

Cora locked the trapdoor and stared at it.

He talked as if they were *friends*, she thought. He wasn't scared. He didn't seem to care that he was tied up; acted like it was some funny misunderstanding. He shouldn't be here, but he seemed harmless, and nice, even…

…And when he'd mentioned living alone, he'd searched

44

her face and tried to steal her secrets.

The snow continued the next morning and the world was white static, even under the camouflage nets. Cora made breakfast and heard Kai's bed creak as he got up.

"Good morning!" he called. He was relentlessly cheerful. She didn't know how to deal with it. "What's for breakfast?"

"Porridge," she replied, and almost slapped her forehead. Now she was answering him! She glowered as she brought it down and refused to respond to his smile, but he didn't seem to mind.

"How's the snow?" he asked as they ate.

"Still heavy."

"If I'd been out there…" He looked serious for a moment. "You saved my life."

"Why were you in that tree?"

"What's your name?" He grinned. "Come on, it's *boring* here. Make something up, I don't care, just give me *something* to call you."

Cora hesitated. "Cora," she said at last.

He smiled. "Hello, Cora," he said, bowing. "I'm Kai."

"Why were you in the tree?"

He laughed. "It's really dull. You'll feel cheated, but … I was looking at other trees. I'm a surveyor."

The word meant nothing to Cora. "Surveyor?" he repeated. "Someone who maps out the land?"

She frowned. "Why?"

"Because of the logging at Recon. There's a big demand for wood, for building in Base, but they've cleared all the nearby trees. They wanted a new place next to the river, so they could float the logs down. I saw somewhere, but I leaned too far over and…" He shrugged. "Then it's all a blur, and I was here."

Cora nodded slowly. That didn't sound good. If they started clearing the woods up around them, there would be more people about.

"So what about you?" asked Kai. "What do you do?"

"Nothing," said Cora. "I live here."

"On your own."

She didn't answer.

"Well," he said. "I'm pleased to meet you, Cora Mountain Girl." He looked around. "So what shall we talk about next?"

Kai chattered endlessly up to Cora as she went about her chores. About surveying, about the weather. About Base – a huge city, with houses and streets, power piped in through special cables, old Glory buildings, schools, markets, government offices, chapels for the Reverents…

At first it washed over her, but she became intrigued as he described the people, the clothes they wore, the way they talked. It felt impossible to imagine so many living together – like a forest of people. And gradually she started answering. Yes, she'd been here for a long time. No, she hadn't been to Recon. Not to Base either, or Sheen. Or anywhere.

"Why do you tap your head like that?" she asked at dinner.

Kai looked up and blinked. "Oh," he laughed. "Force of habit. It's to the Lady Nostic, the Glories. Giving thanks, you know?"

"No." Cora frowned. "Are you a … Reverent, then?"

"I suppose," said Kai. "Isn't everyone?"

"Not us." Seleen had mentioned Reverents before. They were the people who worshipped the Glories. "I think Seleen doesn't like them."

She wasn't sure how she'd come to mention Seleen. Somewhere in Kai's chatter it had just been assumed that he knew that someone else lived there. And then that it was Seleen. It was between descriptions of the great Sanctuary building in Base, or life as a surveyor, or Recon, or the snow, or the thousand other things Kai talked about.

Now Kai put a hand to his heart in mock-horror. "Not

47

like the Reverents? Blasphemy! Why not?"

"I don't know," said Cora. "She doesn't trust them, I think."

He grinned. "I was raised by them, you know. In the orphanage in Base – raised by clerics while you were being raised by wolves. It's pretty much the same but with less howling. Or more, maybe, I dunno. I ran away in the end. I like to keep moving. I was in Sheen too, for a bit."

"What's it like?"

"Sheen?"

"No, being a Reverent."

Kai shrugged. "Boring. It's just all about the Glories – worshipping them, telling us how great they were, and how far we've *fallen*..." He shook his head. "The Seekers are exciting, at least. They're the ones who find old Glory technology and try to make it work. They're always accidentally blowing themselves up. I mean, they're *crazy*. But exciting."

Cora couldn't tell if he was joking.

The snow stopped overnight and by morning the sky was blue, and reflected sunlight flooded the cabin. Cora dug a path from their door and checked the animals. Juliet was indignant, bleating her annoyance. The chickens stayed in their coop and glared at her for opening the door. The air was fresh, and Cora took deep breaths to strip out the dust of being stuck inside for two days. The pass would open soon.

They ate breakfast together in the cellar. Kai was getting adept at eating with his hands tied now. He never complained, which somehow always made Cora feel awkward and apologetic.

"How's your ankle?" she asked.

He flexed it. "Mending, I think. I'll be on my way soon."

Cora nodded. "Oh, I've got your bag," she said suddenly. "Hang on." She fetched it, pulling out the odd black device. "What's this?"

Kai looked delighted. "Fantastic! I didn't know you'd rescued it!" He reached for it, but Cora held back. He grinned. "It's not a weapon. They're binoculars."

Cora frowned. "What's that?"

"Here, I'll show you."

"Tell me."

He sighed. "OK. Well, it's pretty easy. You look through the small end and you can see things far away. Try it."

Cora looked at him. He seemed serious. Cautiously, she peered into the glass circles.

"It's brown," she said.

"You're pointing at the ground. Try moving—"

"Oh!" She realised the brown was actually the dirt cellar floor. As she pointed the device at a corner, it sprang towards her so close that she thought she was about to collide. She took a step back and the room swept dizzyingly about. "Oh!"

"That's it!" said Kai. "Careful. *Please don't drop them.*"

"It's all fuzzy!"

"They're self-focusing," he said. "Just look at one thing for a second; they'll figure it out."

Cora aimed at a patch of brown, and the view shifted to show the wooden shelves at the end of the cellar, as big as if they were right next to her.

"That's *amazing*," she gasped. "How do they work?"

"No idea. How does any Glory tech work? Nobody knows." Kai smiled. "You should try looking outside."

"Could I?"

He laughed and raised his hands. "I can't stop you, can I?"

Cora blushed. "I know, but…"

He shrugged. "Of course." Something seemed to occur to him. "Try looking north."

Cora brought them up and peered through the window with them. It was *incredible*. She could see individual trees from over a kilometre away, the patterns of snow against their bark, trails left by animals…

"I see an owl!" She watched it, tiny and remote, unaware of her.

"Did you look north?" called Kai.

"Hang on. Yes, it's the same! There's the old McKenzie cabin! And there's a kestrel, and—"

"Tell me about the cabin," he interrupted. Cora frowned; something about Kai's voice was different. But she focused back on the cabin.

"It's fallen apart," she said. "Years ago. I never knew them; Seleen said they moved away. I went up there once but…" She remembered looking for a trace of other people; anything to connect to. But the cabin had been stripped bare. "I think the roof's going. And— Oh!"

"What?"

"There's someone there!" Cora's hands shook around the binoculars. "Someone at the cabin!"

"Who is it? Describe them!"

There's someone there! Cora's heart thudded. *More* people! This was terrible!

"Cora!" She realised Kai was standing as close to the trapdoor as his rope stretched, calling. She forced herself to relax.

"Sorry," she muttered. "But someone's there! Hang on."

She looked again. "There's smoke," she said. "And

bags outside. Someone's moving!" A man stepped from the cabin, dressed in a strange outfit, white with black jagged streaks across it. He carried a bag inside. "I think he's moving in!"

"I doubt it," muttered Kai.

"There's another one!" Another man appeared from the cover of the nearby trees, carrying more bags. Cora stared at him, seeming so close, as if he might look up at any moment and see her. The two men chatted. Then they stiffened, turned and each raised a hand to their head.

Out of the trees strode a woman.

She was short, and her clothes were the same as the men's, but very neatly fitting. Her hair was a blonde bob, her skin pale, and somehow Cora knew she was in charge. The men watched her face and nodded as she spoke.

"There's a woman," Cora said. "I think she's their leader."

"What's she doing?"

"Just standing. She's—"

The woman turned and stared at her.

Cora was too far away, even with the binoculars, to see the woman's eyes, but she knew they were staring right at her. They bored into her as if memorising every detail of her face, her clothes, everything she thought, and Cora looked back helplessly. The woman couldn't possibly see her; she was ten kilometres away at least, under camouflage. But it made no difference. She was pinned.

The woman's gaze moved on.

Cora felt as if her knees were turning to liquid. She wanted to stop looking, but didn't dare.

"Cora? What is it?"

"There's…" She coughed. She couldn't explain how scared she had been. "The woman. I thought she… She's…"

"Sisal," said Kai softly. "Her name is Sisal."

Dice

"Sisal's the head of Protection," said Kai. "Thorsen's deputy."

The binoculars hung around Cora's neck and she found herself touching them as if for comfort. She had a constant urge to go up and check on the strangers, as if only by watching could she make sure they didn't find the cabin. But she felt that if she tried to look at the woman, she would know; she would sense Cora across the hillside...

"Who's Thorsen?" she asked.

Kai blinked at her. "Huh. Really?"

"What?"

He shook his head. "Sorry. I mean, you're up here, you wouldn't know. Look. All this – Recon, Sheen, Base – is Colony, yes? The whole world."

Cora nodded. "Yes, of course."

"And Governor Thorsen runs it."

"How?"

Kai shrugged. "Well, it's a democracy, so, you know, we vote him in – we all decide he should be in charge. And then he controls where to build, and what laws there should be, stuff like that."

"OK."

"And Sisal is the head of Protection. Her job is to keep Colony safe from criminals, terrorists, whatever."

"Terrorists?"

Kai smiled. "Well, some folks aren't too thrilled with Thorsen. They want to get rid of him."

"But couldn't they vote him out?" asked Cora, frowning.

The boy nodded. "Sure. But Thorsen runs Colony, and Sisal works for Thorsen and makes sure the voting is done properly. And maybe, if it seems like you're going to vote the wrong way, Sisal helps *persuade* you. She protects us from criminals and terrorists … and from people who don't quite think how Thorsen wants them to."

Cora tried to understand. "But then how do you change governors?"

Kai laughed. "With great difficulty! Thorsen's been in power for fifteen years, and Sisal's run Protection the whole time. He keeps winning the votes. Everybody loves him." He shrugged. "If they know what's good for them.

"Sisal arrived in Recon a couple of weeks ago." He looked serious for a moment. "She started in the town and then went off into the hills. When I was surveying, I saw soldiers up by that cabin and I guessed it was her. She almost never leaves Base, and everyone's wondering what's going on. They say she's searching for someone." He glanced at Cora. "Any idea who?"

Cora shook her head. "No."

Kai shrugged. "Well, whoever it is, she seems to think they're on the other side of the valley. Which is good, because Sisal's a scary woman." Again he glanced at her, and again Cora refused to make eye contact.

"I'll get lunch," she said.

She spent the afternoon making sure the netting and fences were still standing after the snowfall. Everything seemed fine. The chickens started venturing out into their area, now scraped clear, and Juliet munched at any grass that poked through.

Cora kept the binoculars with her and pointed them at the faraway cabin again and again. The two men were assembling something, though she couldn't tell what. It had three large metal legs and looked like a Glory device. Even from this distance she could *feel* the care that they were taking with it.

"Who were the Glories?" she asked Kai later.

"What?"

"They're setting up a Glory device. And you've got these." She held up the binoculars. "We call them Glory things, but why? Who are the Glories? You say the Reverents worship them. You talk about them like everyone knows, but I don't."

He looked at her in surprise. "Really?" Cora shook her head, and he whistled. "Huh." He sat back against the wall and thought. "Well, I suppose no one knows for sure. But I know what the Reverents say, and what most folk believe. They say they came from the stars."

Cora frowned. "What?"

Kai shrugged. "The story is that the stars are actually worlds like ours, but far away. And they *say* that one of them is where the Glories live. And that in the beginning they came here and found us humans, and looked after us."

"Why?"

He shrugged again. "No idea. We don't know much about them. They made themselves look like us – like humans, but perfect. And they had these amazing powers. They could talk to each other with their minds, talk to machines, fly…

"They built all of Colony – Base first, and then

Sheen, Recon, a couple of other places. They made incredible things, like the binoculars, and power cells. Impossible things. And the Lady Nostic looked after them."

"The Lady Nostic was a Glory?"

"Maybe. Or maybe something else. There's a big religious debate about it; it's very dull." He sighed. "Anyway, they came, they built Colony, and then they left."

"Why?"

"Nobody knows. Bored, maybe? *I'd* leave, if I could."

"And the Reverents worship them even though they've gone?"

"Oh, *yeah*." Kai grinned. "They're sure they'll come back one day to *saaaaaave* us." He shrugged. "Most folk don't. But we all do the festivals, and we all give thanks to the Lady Nostic. I guess we're all believers, really."

"Not us," said Cora. Seleen had never mentioned a festival. She hardly mentioned the Glories at all. Cora had always felt she disapproved of them; impressive, flashy but ultimately unreliable.

"Yeah, not you," agreed Kai. He gave her a curious look. "I wonder why?"

At sunset, Cora checked every shutter, twice, before

turning the lights on. Later, when it was completely dark, she switched the lights off, opened one shutter and stared out at the hillside. She waited for several minutes, gazing into the black void, until – *there!* – she saw a tiny flicker of yellow, kilometres away. Someone opening the door to their cabin; perhaps going to relieve themselves. She waited another minute and saw the flicker again as they returned. She closed the shutters.

The next day was the same.

Cora knew they couldn't see the cabin. The camouflage netting was interwoven with ivy and branches from living trees, green in the summer and snow-covered now, invisible from fifty metres. They lit no fires, made no paths. Even so, every time she watched them, Cora's heart thudded in her throat.

When would the snow clear and the pass reopen? Was Seleen on her way back? Recon was on the other side of the ridge, and Cora didn't dare go up there to look. That evening, dinner was quiet. She served up two bowls of soup without speaking, and ignored Kai as she ate. The boy was also quiet for once, thinking his own thoughts.

"Hey," he said at last. Cora looked up, and he smiled. "Enough brooding, eh?"

Cora stood and shook herself. "Yes," she said briskly. "Bowl."

He handed it over. "Want a game of something?"

"A game?"

"You know, something for fun."

Cora frowned. "We don't really play games."

"Yeah, it's a real party round here," he drawled. "I've got some dice in my bag. You ever play dice?"

Cora shook her head and searched through his pack until she found the pouch of small white cubes she'd seen earlier.

"That's them," he said, reaching for them. Cora hesitated, but they were just cubes carved from bone, with gold dots on each side. She handed over the pouch and he smiled, poured them into his hand and rolled them between his palms. They made a pleasing, clacking sound.

"These are dice," he said. "The dots are values, and if I roll them…"

He shook the cubes and threw them on to the ground.

"…I get a score. Like this – that's three fives. You play dice by betting on these scores." He shrugged. "Normally you bet for money, but we'll need something else. Do you have anything we could use as counters?"

Cora fetched a jar of dried beans, and Kai counted

some out. "This is your money," he said. He sorted through the dice and put one back in the pouch. "Not this one," he murmured with an odd smile. "This one's not for friends." Cora didn't know what he meant by that. He put four dice into her empty cup and four into his own.

"We shake like this," he said, putting his hand over the top and shaking the cup, "and roll." He flipped the cup upside down on the ground, with the dice hidden inside. Then he carefully lifted it, so that Cora couldn't see, and peered inside. Cora dutifully rattled her own cup and turned it over, and peered. She had two fives, a three and a one.

"Now I'm going to make a claim," said Kai. "I'll say I have two fours, OK?" Cora nodded. "You have to make a *better* claim – either three fours, or two fives, something like that."

"I have two fives," she said. "And a three and a one."

He smiled. "Well, good! But this is a *secrets* game. You don't tell me what you really have. You make a *claim*. Understand?"

Cora didn't, but nodded.

"Actually," Kai said, "I have three sixes."

Cora frowned. "But if you have two fours, you can't have three sixes as well."

"Well, if you think I'm lying, then you *call*," said Kai.

"Call," she said. Kai lifted the cup. Two fours, a five and a three looked up at her, and she beamed in satisfaction.

"Well done!" said Kai. "You win a bean. Want to play again?"

Cora shrugged. "Sure."

She did well. Dice was a simple game. Gradually she got used to the idea of lying, though it seemed wrong – not immoral, more like there was something *undoing* about describing the dice wrongly. But she was good at spotting Kai's lies.

"It's just probability," she said, collecting another bean. "The chance of you really having three sixes was only zero point zero-one-six-two."

Kai's eyebrows lifted. "You worked that out just now?"

"I'm good with numbers."

"Hmm." He poked forlornly at his dwindling pile of beans. "How about giving me the chance to win some back?"

"How?"

"Well… Suppose, when I make a claim, I can raise the bet, if I think I've got a good hand?"

Cora grinned. "Sure, why not?"

Thirty minutes later, she stared at the six remaining beans in her pile in despair.

Everything had gone wrong! Kai bet on hands that

62

couldn't exist, bet high when she *knew* he couldn't have the dice to back it up. But somehow, whenever she challenged, there they were. And when she didn't, she lost. And any time she herself ever, tentatively, tried to lie, he pounced, raising his own bet and forcing her to match, and calling just when she thought she had him.

"How do you *know*?" she demanded.

He grinned and pulled more winnings towards his overflowing pile. "Instincts."

"But I did everything right! I made a false claim, and then a real one, and—"

"I could just tell," he said. "It's a knack."

Cora picked up a die. "How do you make them be what you want? Are you…" *Cheating*, she wanted to say, but didn't.

Kai hesitated. "Perhaps we should stop. It's only a game. Just beans, right?"

"One more round," said Cora.

He shrugged and nodded. "One more, then."

They rolled, and Cora glanced at her dice. *Four fives!* She bit her lip and tried to stay calm. He couldn't beat her. He'd need four sixes – the odds were almost thirteen-hundred to one!

She coughed and said, "Two fours. And, I, um, bet an extra bean."

Kai studied her. "Three fours."

"Three fives. And another bean."

"Three sixes," he said. "And raise you another bean."

"Four fives and two more beans!" Cora grinned, pushing her last two beans into the pot.

"Four sixes," said Kai. "And one more bean."

Cora stopped. "But I don't have any more," she said with dismay.

He shrugged. "Then you can't make the bet."

"But I'm going to win!"

"Not if you can't make the bet." Kai sighed. "Unless you bet with something else…"

"Yes!" Cora frowned. "Like what?"

Kai pursed his lips together, thinking. "Like … a secret, maybe? One secret for a bean."

Cora stared at her cup. "I can't do that."

Kai shrugged. "OK."

"But I was going to *win*!" Cora looked at Kai. He wasn't smiling now. His face was blank, no expression; just waiting.

"All right," she said defiantly. "I *call*." She grinned. "Show me those four sixes then!"

Kai sighed and looked down. "Huh."

Then he lifted his cup and four sixes looked up at Cora.

Cora stared. "What? No!"

The triumph she'd been feeling a moment ago twisted into a horrible, sick feeling. "No. No, that's not possible."

Kai shrugged. "Lucky roll."

"But you were *bluffing*!" she protested.

"Not this time," he said. "Sorry."

"But that's…" Her blood fizzed. "Stupid!" she shouted. "Stupid game!"

He didn't respond to that. Instead, he said calmly, "You owe me a secret."

"But I didn't think you were going to win!"

"Well, obviously. But I did, and you owe me a secret. And the secret I want, Cora, is: *why are you two hiding on this mountain?*"

Cora leapt to her feet. "You *cheated*!"

"I didn't."

"You made me bet!"

"No, I—"

"Shut up!" She stomped back up the ladder.

"Cora, I promise—"

"Shut up!"

She slammed the trapdoor shut, locked it, sat on her bed and fumed.

Actions

Later, Cora lay in bed, still awake, still furious.

How had he done it? She thought of her accusation – *you made me bet!* – and felt a hot flush of embarrassment. Of course he hadn't. She'd done it herself, and he'd let her, knowing he was going to win. But *how*? How had he rolled those sixes?

There was a thin line of light coming through the trapdoor; when she'd stormed out she'd left the lamp on down there. She gazed at it, and eventually cursed, crept across and peered through the gap.

Kai was asleep and snoring. Cora watched him for a while, then crept down the ladder and knelt in front of the dice still scattered on the floor. She examined them. He had to have cheated – but how? She glanced at Kai, still asleep, and thought for a moment. Then she let her mind drift backwards in time … and *looked*.

She found the moment where Kai had lifted his cup to reveal the dice, and saw the hundreds of tiny events leading to that point. The sixes had appeared because… Well, because he'd lifted the cup, of course. Cora worked back. He'd lifted the cup because Cora had called. She'd called because he'd offered to let her bet with secrets…

Step by step, she watched the game in reverse. And gradually, to her astonishment, she realised that she'd been right – he *had* made her bet. He'd tricked her with his play – with a hundred tiny actions; he'd made her confident, then overconfident. A slight pause, a look of resignation, a tremor as he raised the bid… Little by little, he'd manipulated her.

Cora leaned back in shock. It was like a physical attack – he'd done this *to her*, on purpose! Furious, she refocused and *looked* again, back to the moment where he'd peeked under his cup for the first time, seen his dice roll…

Four sixes.

He'd actually rolled it. He hadn't cheated – it had just happened, at just the right time. He'd rolled a good hand – the best possible hand – but the key to this game wasn't the dice rolls, it was the *betting*. So he'd steered Cora into betting too much, with little false messages. Little lies.

She realised she was gripping the dice so tight that they dug into her palm. Hot embarrassment pounded at her temples. She forced herself to relax, and let one die roll out of her hand, on to the ground. It landed three-up. She *watched* it – saw the muscles in her hand move, saw the tiny bounces before it came to rest, held them in her mind…

And this was the other thing she could do.

Delicately, carefully, Cora imagined a change. She imagined that the muscles in her hand moved just a tiny bit faster, *there*. She saw in her mind the consequences of this minute change, blooming out like a flower unfurling – the die tumbling from her hand in a very slightly different direction, bouncing a very slightly different way…

Five.

Not that change then. Discarding it, she drifted back, imagined a different version again. The muscle trembled. The die landed…

Six.

The new timeline drifted in Cora's mind's eye, the changes like threads in a breeze. She gathered them together in her mind and when she had them, held every consequence clear…

She *fixed* them into place.

Reality re-flowed. The die fell, landed, bounced, stopped, and six gold dots looked up at her.

Cora blew out a trembling breath.

In her mind she saw both realities; the one where she had rolled a three, and this new one. The old reality faded out of existence and the new one took over. She had rolled a six.

She rolled another die. This came up a six all by itself, and Cora smiled a small, grim smile, and rolled the next one. Four. She went to work again.

The dice were easy to deal with, in a way. They had clear outcomes; one of six results. She just had to tweak things until they came up correctly.

Two.

Three.

Six.

Still, it was a strain. Anything beyond a day was impossible to see, and she couldn't change events further than a few hours back. And the more consequences there were, the harder it was to keep track of them. The fourth die came down and she tracked it, and tweaked it, and rewrote its history over and over until at last it landed the way she wanted, and *fixed* it.

Four sixes.

There. If she'd done that in the game, she wouldn't have lost. If she could do it every time, she would have *won*, despite Kai's deceit. Cora smiled, but it was a rueful smile. She couldn't actually do that. She could *fix* one die roll at a time, right here, with no one watching – the odds were only one in six. To change all four, all at once, was too hard to imagine.

She noticed Kai's bag and the one remaining die – the one Kai had said he wouldn't use. It seemed identical to the others, but for a tiny nick on one face. *This one's not for friends*, he'd said. Curious, Cora rolled it, and it came up with a one.

Again, she slipped into *looking*, followed the die back along its history, watched it moving and tumbling. She imagined the die bouncing in its new, subtly different way, and the effects billowed out…

One again.

She released this line and imagined a different change.

Two.

And again.

One.

Three.

One.

There was something wrong with this die. It was weighted in some way; it *wanted* to land on one. Cora felt a pressure in her mind, like the edge of a migraine. She should stop and wait to recover, but she kept going out of frustration. A tiny prickle of sweat itched against her forehead.

70

Stop, she thought, but didn't. She replayed the die's bounce over and over, tried moving further back in time, until the realities started to overlap, too complex to keep track. The pressure was a sharp throbbing pain now, and then...

An image appeared in her mind's eye, of a face. It seemed to float in front of her, a calm face, a woman with smooth brown skin and short black hair. The woman from Cora's half-remembered dreams – but not a dream, almost real this time. She had an expression of mild concern. She was speaking, but Cora couldn't hear.

Six.

At last! With all the threads of reality held together, Cora *fixed*, saw the six and slumped in exhaustion.

That was so *foolish*, she thought. What had possessed her to stretch herself like that? She'd never done anything so hard before. The other dice had been relatively easy, but in her anger she'd been sucked into trying this one again and again, even when she *knew* it was different, even when she knew it didn't want to land the right way. Foolish.

And whose face was it, so strange, but so familiar? How could she be there; how could Cora see her? Why did Cora feel she should *know* her? She'd seemed worried. What had she been trying to say?

71

None of it made sense. What just happened?

"What just happened?" asked Kai.

Cora leapt back in alarm. Kai was awake and staring at the die.

"Nothing!" she stammered. "Just dice!"

Kai moved his head from side to side, peering at it from different angles. "It was a one," he muttered. "I saw it."

"No! You're mistaken. It's a six, see—"

"No." Kai gazed at her, his normally cheerful face absolutely serious, his mouth fixed. "It was a one."

"You mustn't tell!" she blurted, and then could have slapped herself. "I mean…" Then she fled back up the ladder and slammed the trapdoor shut, and stood above it in the dark, trembling. *He saw it. He saw it!*

"It was amazing!" he called up. "I won't tell, I promise! Just show me what you did!"

Cora bit her lip and then slowly opened the trapdoor again. Kai was standing as close as he could get at the end of the rope, staring at her.

"You can't tell anyone," she croaked.

He nodded. "Of course."

"*Promise.*"

"OK, I promise! I swear by the Lady Nostic!"

"If Seleen finds out…" Cora grimaced. "You don't

want that, *ever*. Understand?"

Kai nodded again.

Still Cora wavered. But Kai's astonishment was quite … *pleasing*, in a way, she realised. Seleen had refused to talk about it, like a shameful secret, but this boy wanted to know.

"It's a thing I can do," she said. She felt a sudden thrill at saying the words out loud. "I can see … back. When things happen, I can see what caused them. Not very far; about a day. When the die lands, I can see what affected it: the throw, the air moving, the way it bounced. Everything that led to that number.

"And sometimes … for tiny things…" She drew a breath. "I can change them."

Kai blinked. "You can make it be a six?"

"No. I can't just make it be what I want. But I can change tiny things, and see what would happen, and then I can *fix* them like that."

"That's just…" Kai shook his head and picked up a die. "You could have changed the dice in the game," he said. "To have four sixes, like me."

Cora shook her head. "I can't *make* it be four sixes. All I can do is replay the roll over and over in my head. One die, that's a one in six chance. For four in one throw, I'd need to replay a thousand times, maybe. I can't do that, it's too hard. And it takes time while I'm doing it, at least until I *fix* things."

Kai nodded. "OK." Then he frowned. "Does it work with people?"

"What? No!" gasped Cora. "No! I mean— I mean, yes, but I'd never, Seleen would never…" She couldn't even find words to describe how bad that would be. "No, *never* people!"

"But you could make me forget. Or you could change things so I never saw you?"

"Yes, but I wouldn't—"

"And I'd never know. Or would I still remember?"

Cora sighed. "You'd remember something, for a few seconds. When it affects you, you see it. That's how you knew the die had changed. You'd probably think it was a dream or something. But it doesn't matter – I *couldn't*."

Above her, Juliet was bleating. It was nearly morning. "I have to go," she said. Terrified realisation suddenly washed over her. What had she done?

"Yes, but—"

"I have to go!"

She scrambled back up the ladder, locked the trapdoor and left. Her heart was thudding. What had she *done*?

At breakfast, Kai watched her as if she might suddenly

74

burst into flames or shatter in front of him. He didn't seem scared though. Cora thought that was because he hadn't met Seleen.

"How long have you been able to do it?" he asked as they ate.

Cora hesitated. But she'd already told him everything else, hadn't she? "A few years. First I could see, then … change things. Tiny things; dust. But over the last couple of years, a bit more."

He nodded. "Can Seleen do it?"

"No."

"And your parents?"

"I don't know. But Seleen…" Cora tried to think how to describe it. It wasn't that Seleen had known she could do it. But she hadn't been surprised. "I think she knew something was going to happen."

"And that's why she keeps you up here."

Cora frowned. "This is just where we live."

"Locked away out of sight."

"No, that's not how it is. We just keep to ourselves."

"Uh-huh." He leaned back and examined her. "You know, the Reverents would do almost anything to meet you." He smiled. "They'd probably worship you. How would you like that?"

"What?"

"Well, you know what it is, don't you? This thing you can do?"

Cora shook her head. "No?"

Kai finished his bowl. "Glory powers." He looked at her. "That's what you've got. You're like the Glories."

"What? No!"

"Of course!" he said. "I mean, that's what they'll say, right? They're *always* looking for stuff like this."

Cora stared at him in horror. "You mustn't tell, you understand? You *mustn't*."

He shrugged. "Look, it's none of my business. We're all just trying to get by, right? I like an easy life. I've no interest in getting tangled up with any of this." He grinned. "They'd make me go back to *church*, Cora. I'm not doing that!"

She looked at him, biting her lip. He seemed sincere. She nodded and took the tray.

Upstairs, she soaked the bowls and stared out of the window towards the tiny cottage far to the north. Without Kai's binoculars it was almost invisible, just a smudge through a tiny gap in the netting.

What was she going to do? Could she trust him? No. And yet, he seemed… What would Seleen say?

"Could I have a cup of tea?" he called up. "And some of that disgusting goat's milk." Despite herself, Cora smiled. She had to admit, it was quite nice having him around. He was different to Seleen, less stressful. It was … interesting. The water boiled and Cora poured, adding a spoonful of tea leaves to each cup, and milk.

"Here," she called. "Lovely goat's milk, just for you—"

Footsteps crunched outside and the outer door rattled, and Cora turned in shock. The inside door opened and a large, hooded figure stood in the doorway.

"Hey," said Seleen.

Consequences

Seleen was wrapped in a heavy jacket, and her leggings and boots were caked in snow. She lowered her backpack to the floor with a sigh.

"Hey," she said again.

Cora stared at her. Seleen peeled off her scarf and nodded to the cups. "How did you know I was coming?" She looked at the open trapdoor, and the wooden batons nailed over it. "What's this?"

"I—"

"Hey, where's my cup of tea?" called Kai.

Seleen froze. She stared at the trapdoor, then at Cora. "What's this?" Her voice was flat and cold.

Cora shook her head. "It's OK! It's just a boy. He was hurt in the woods—"

"Hello? Hello there?"

"He's injured his ankle. He's just here until he can

78

walk again…"

Seleen looked at her, and Cora's words dried up. Somehow Seleen was holding a knife now. Cora hadn't even seen her move, but there it was, glinting and deadly.

"He's tied up," tried Cora.

Without a word, Seleen stepped to the trapdoor and peered down.

"Hello," said Kai, smiling up at her. "You must be Seleen?"

"Get back," Seleen said. Her voice was still flat. "Back against the far wall."

"It's OK," he said. "I promise I'm not a threat—"

"*Now*." She gestured with the knife and his smile faded.

"Sure, OK! Here I go, look!" He limped to the back wall and held up his hands, still tied together. "See, nothing to worry about."

Seleen jumped through the hole and landed without stumbling. She checked the rope around his wrists and followed it up to the hook in the ceiling.

"How long has he been here?" she asked.

"Just a few days," said Kai. "I fell, and—"

"Shut up."

"Five days," said Cora, climbing down behind her. "He was in the upper woods. He fell out of a tree and sprained his ankle."

Seleen glanced at Kai's bandages. "And you … *know* he fell out of the tree?"

Cora bit her lip. "Yes."

Seleen nodded at Kai. "What were you doing there?"

"Surveying," said Kai. "They're looking for a place for a logging camp. I thought there might be a stream up here."

Seleen frowned. "There's nothing like that around here."

"Actually, there's a channel that cuts down—"

"*No*," said Seleen. She leaned towards him. "There's *nothing like that around here.*"

Kai stared into her eyes and swallowed. "I, ah, yeah, there's nothing. That's what I'll say. Definitely."

Seleen glared at him for a few seconds longer, then nodded to his ankle.

"That looks mended to me," she said. "The pass is clear; if you set off now you could be in Recon before dark. Show me your hands."

Kai held them out, and with one swift slice, almost too fast for Cora to see, Seleen whipped her knife up through the cords that tied them together. Kai flinched.

"Get your things and go," she said.

He nodded. "Sure." He rubbed his wrists. "Listen, thanks for everything—"

80

"*Now.*"

"OK! OK, I'm going." He put his boots on, wincing as he pulled the left one over his injured ankle. Then he gathered his coat and his bag, edged around Seleen, nodded to Cora and climbed the ladder. Cora and Seleen followed him.

He found the front door and peered out. "I, ah, don't know which way," he muttered.

Seleen pointed down the hill with her knife. "Keep under tree cover as far as you can, then turn left when you get to that rock. See it?" Kai looked at the blade, close to his face, and nodded, gulping.

"Thanks," he said. "Cora saved my life—"

"You need to know this about me," growled Seleen. "I'm good at finding people. If you ever mention her name, or say anything about us, or this place, I'll find *you*. Understand?"

He swallowed. "Yes. Absolutely. No problem. Yes."

"Go."

He looked from her to Cora and seemed about to say something. But instead he turned and limped down the hill.

Seleen and Cora watched him until he disappeared under the trees, then Seleen slammed the door. Anger radiated from her like heat.

"What have I told you?" she asked. Her voice was low. Cora sighed. "He was hurt—"

"*What have I told you?*" Seleen spun. "How could you be so *stupid?*"

"He was *hurt!*" snapped Cora. "He was *dying!*"

"That's not our problem!"

Cora threw her arms up. "You're saying you'd have let him *die?*"

"I'm saying it's not our problem! We stay out of the way, we don't get involved, we live our own life."

Cora almost laughed. "What life? *This?* I never do anything! Kai told me about *real* life – about Base, about people!"

"This is the only way to survive," said Seleen. "I swore to your parents I would keep you *safe*. I've spent thirteen years looking after you—"

"You keep me here because *you're* scared!"

"Yes, I am!" snarled Seleen. "You used your powers, didn't you? While I was gone? You *changed* something!"

"What?" Cora faltered. "No."

Seleen nodded in grim satisfaction. "Yes. *That's* why we stay here. Because you can't follow the simplest, most important rule. *That's* why I came back today. *That's* why I walked all night – because you can't be trusted!"

"You don't trust *anyone!*"

"You *can't* trust anyone!" shouted Seleen. "Government, Reverents, strangers, friends, *no one*. They'll use you. Friends betray you. The ones you love *leave* you!"

She shook her head in disgust. "Enough of this. I have work to do." She pulled a fresh power cell from her pack and went outside, slamming the door. Cora heard her open the generator cover with a clatter. After a little while, the lights dipped and then came back, as the new cell started up.

They prowled around each other all day. Cora stayed inside, clearing and mending. Seleen checked the fences, then climbed up on to the roof to make repairs, then clattered in the basement. At dinner they ate silently. Afterwards, Seleen stood at the window and glared out at the hillside.

Eventually Cora said, "I'm sorry."

Seleen sniffed. "Yup."

Then she pulled on her thick coat, picked up the toolbox and went back outside, leaving Cora ready to spit in fury.

That evening, Cora lay in her bunk and fumed. At Seleen, holding her in this cabin, controlling her life. At Kai; smiling, funny, charming, untrustworthy Kai.

And at herself, for being so easily manipulated. For telling Kai about her powers. To – what? – impress him? For confirming Seleen's constant belief that she couldn't be trusted.

The ones you love leave you. She thought about Seleen's words. As a child, it had never occurred to her to wonder where Seleen had been before the cabin. The idea of her having a previous life was disturbing. *You can't trust anyone.* For the first time, Cora wondered – could she trust Seleen?

But that was too much. It was like not knowing whether to trust gravity. So instead Cora thought about the dice, tumbling over and over. She'd never made so many changes before. It had hurt, like pressure in her mind. And then that strange moment, seeing the face…

Whose face? No one she knew, but it seemed so *familiar*. The face from her drawings, her dreams, like someone she'd known her whole life. And the words she'd been saying; Cora could almost hear them. And the sense of warning. Who was she, this woman who looked nothing like her, and yet…?

Cora fell asleep.

—And awoke, suddenly aware – without knowing how – that something was moving outside the cabin.

The world was black, with only a glimmer of moonlight,

and completely silent. Cora lay frozen, listening.

There.

A soft, swishing noise, like the wind through trees, but too close. Not grass either. A wolf? But Seleen had fixed the fence, and the chickens were quiet. And the sound had been artificial, somehow. Not soft. Something hard, covered up.

Cora's heart beat faster. Someone creeping up. Should she move? Wake Seleen? Or pretend to still be asleep? Were they already watching? She opened her mouth—

—And a hand clamped against her face, pushing her down into her bunk. A metal blade grated close to her ear, and before she could struggle or even react, a voice, low and hissing, said:

"Keep quiet."

It was Seleen.

She was dressed in dark mottled clothes, her deep-brown skin merged with shadows, and the only thing Cora could see clearly was her eyes, and the faintest glint of her knife. She was looking insistently at Cora.

Cora gave a careful nod and Seleen moved her hand. She put one finger to her lips and listened. After a moment, she pointed three fingers towards the door. Then a pause. Then two fingers towards the back door.

Three at the front, two at the back.

Cora wanted to ask *who*. She could make out a small scratching sound at the front. Someone was trying to open the door.

Seleen put her mouth close to Cora's ear. "When I move," she breathed, "head for the cellar."

Cora nodded.

The door creaked faintly, then stopped. Then – slowly – it creaked again. Seleen lifted a small device, a black box with two covered switches on the top. Carefully, she opened the cover to the first switch.

"Close your eyes," she whispered. Cora did so. The door creaked again. She heard a click—

And then a sound like a huge piece of paper ripping in two, and a light pressed hard against her eyelids leaving a savage red glow, and a grunt, and a heavy thud—

—And Seleen's hand shaking her shoulder, hard, *NOW!* Cora scrambled out of bed and towards the cellar trapdoor. As she ran, she saw the intruders.

There were three of them, in black outfits with face masks and goggles. They lay on the floor in a heap. Two were struggling to get free, but the one on top wasn't moving. Above them, the eaves of the cabin burned with a shocking white light that seemed to fizz. *That's where Seleen was fixing the roof,* Cora thought.

Seleen shoved her towards the trapdoor. As she tugged

at the handle another voice came from the back of the cabin, with an odd crackly twang to it. It was shouting,

"*GO-GO-GO!*"

Something crashed through the window and landed in front of them with a clunk. It looked like a hard metal ball, about the size of Cora's fist.

"GET DOWN!" roared Seleen. She ran *towards* the ball and kicked it against the far corner of the cabin. Just before it hit the wall it blinked, and the air around it *rippled*—

A silent, invisible hand picked Cora up, threw her past the trapdoor and dumped her hard against the floor. Her head rang. Vaguely she looked up and saw Seleen tumbling next to her, and the two struggling men at the front door slapped back down.

And two more, climbing through the rear windows.

There are two more. The thought spun in her head uselessly, pushing everything else out. Beside her, Seleen groaned, then reached for the trapdoor handle and heaved it open.

"*In,*" she grunted. Cora looked at her, baffled. *There are two more*, she tried to say, but her mouth wouldn't move.

"*In!*" snarled Seleen. She grabbed Cora's arm and dragged her, and with a shout of alarm Cora tumbled down the steps and crashed on to the packed-earth floor.

Seleen was above her, silhouetted in flames. She flung her hand out, throwing the knife, then leapt down after Cora and slammed the trapdoor shut behind her, flicking the light switch on. There were new bolts on the inside; Seleen locked them and crouched down beside Cora.

"You OK?" she shouted. Cora tried to focus on her.

What?

"ARE. YOU. HURT?"

There are two more. Cora shook her head. Footsteps thudded above them and someone tried to open the trapdoor. Seleen dragged Cora to her feet and towards the back of the cellar, to a large stack of shelves where they kept winter supplies. Seleen reached up and, with a heave, tipped the shelves over. Behind them was a hatch. Seleen opened it to reveal a narrow tunnel.

"In!" she shouted, and hoisted Cora up. Cora stumbled and crawled into the tiny space. Behind her she heard splintering wood and a roar. Seleen crawled in after her.

The tunnel was too small for them to move quickly. Cora was still in her vest and shorts, and rock scraped against her legs. They were too slow. The intruders were coming down the steps. They were too *slow*.

"Seleen!" she screamed.

"Keep moving!" shouted Seleen, and pulled the hatch closed behind them. It was pitch black, then a faint light glimmered behind Cora. Straining, she looked back and saw the light was coming off the tiny device in Seleen's hand. Seleen lifted the lid off the second switch.

"Cover your ears!" she shouted.

She flicked the switch.

Recon

The tunnel was so dark that Cora couldn't even see the end until she banged against it.

"It's blocked," she called behind her. Her voice quivered. The air was hot, almost unbreathable, and dank sweaty earth pressed against her on all sides. "I can't move; it's blocked."

"It's a cover," came Seleen's voice. "Just push through."

Cora heaved, and a faint glimmer of light appeared, and a blessed rush of freezing air. With another heave the cover fell off, and she crawled out into a tiny clearing.

An orange glow flickered behind them – the cabin, on fire. The air was raw. Cora shivered and found it hard to stop. Seleen cast about under a nearby mass of snowy thorn bushes and recovered two backpacks. Reaching into one, she pulled out clothes and boots for Cora.

"We have to keep moving," she said. "Get dressed."

Cora gaped at her. "What happened?" she managed. Her ears were still ringing from the explosion. "I mean – what *happened* there?"

Seleen shrugged. "We got lucky. Ready to move?" Cora dragged her boots on and nodded. Seleen examined her. "You feeling dizzy? Having trouble breathing?"

"Yes."

"You're in shock. You'll probably be sick. Try not to get any on your clothes."

She strode out of the glade and down into the woods. Cora rubbed her hands against her face as if clearing away cobwebs, and then followed.

When she threw up a few minutes later, she was careful to avoid her shoes.

Seleen carried both packs and walked quickly, and Cora had to trot to keep up. It left her no time to think. All her attention was on trying not to be sick again, and controlling the tremors that shook her body. Eventually Seleen stopped at a clearing near the bottom of the wood. Behind them, the cabin was still burning, though not fiercely.

"This will do," said Seleen. She pulled a small heater from her pack, and a sheet of tenting, and made a quick shelter against a tree. "We can't stay for long, but you need to warm up."

Cora gratefully crawled under the canvas and pushed her hands against the heater. They sat for a short while in silence. "These are my clothes," said Cora eventually.

Seleen raised an eyebrow. Cora said, "You must have packed them recently."

"Yes."

Cora nodded. "And you were dressed, even your boots."

"Yes."

"You knew they were coming. Because of Kai."

Seleen shrugged and handed her a tin mug of hot, sweet tea, and Cora sipped at it. Her bones warmed, and her hands stopped trembling, but there was still a strange blankness whenever she tried to think. She shook her head.

"You said we were lucky."

Seleen nodded. "Lucky I had time to prepare. They were good, and they had Glory technology. Night goggles, stun grenades... Expensive stuff, irreplaceable. Experienced agents, with back-up; you could hear it on the radio—" She stopped and cursed. "I should have taken a radio," she muttered, shaking her head. "Getting stupid in my old age."

Cora said, "You think it *was* Kai?"

"Don't know. He'd have to reach Recon, they'd have

to get all the way up here in time…" Seleen frowned. "I don't know."

Cora closed her eyes. "I didn't tell you about the woman."

Seleen looked up. "What?"

"At the McKenzie cabin. A woman and two men, maybe more. She was… Kai said she was called Sisal."

Seleen stared. "Sisal."

"I'm sorry, I should have said, but she went away over the ridge and I thought she'd gone. I didn't know she was looking for *us*."

Seleen rubbed her forehead. "Yes. She was looking for us." She glowered into her mug. Cora thought about the way the woman had seemed to stare into her, even from the far mountainside, like a hawk.

Oh.

She managed to make it out of the tent before she was sick again. Behind her, Seleen sighed. "I'll make some more tea, then."

An hour later they set off again. It was still dark, and the cabin was a dim red glow behind them. Seleen led them down towards Recon.

"We've got power cells, a tent, a heater, and food supplies for two weeks," she said. "We can hide in the forest. But I need to know how many there are, and where they've searched already. I'll find out in Recon."

Cora nodded and concentrated on following. The second mug of tea sat in her stomach like a lump of stone, but she no longer felt she was going to bring it back up, and the blankness in her mind had faded a little. But as it faded, guilt took its place. She'd brought Kai into their cabin. She'd let him see her using her powers. She'd seen Sisal on the hillside and not said anything because … what? Because she'd been angry? Seleen had been right all along. Whoever had done this, it was because of Cora.

This was her fault.

So she didn't complain when Seleen upped the pace, didn't ask to stop though her legs burned. Carried her backpack, followed obediently and resisted any temptation to try to *look*, to see what had happened … and who had betrayed them.

They stopped around noon and set up the makeshift tent, chewed on thin ration strips and then slept for a few hours until dark. Then Seleen led them down the last stretch, into the town of Recon.

Despite the situation, Cora was excited to see the town, and stared about as they entered. It was warmer down here, and the snow petered out as they passed the first few farm steadings; the grass underfoot became a muddy trail, and then a cobbled path, and brick houses replaced the steadings, dozens of them. There was a buzz of ozone in the air, and a strange combination of smells – cooking, food waste, wood smoke, a harsh odour of tar, the oily tang of machinery. There were no people around, but Cora could tell they were near. Faint light leaked through the shutters of the nearby buildings, and she imagined the humans inside, tens of them, *hundreds...* Her heart thudded.

Seleen led her carefully down narrow lanes, avoiding the wider streets. There was noise up ahead, conversations and shouting, and the busy sound of work, and when they reached the centre of Recon, Seleen stopped behind a stack of pallets, put her finger to her lips and peered into the central square.

There was the old Recon tower, closer than Cora had ever seen it before, gleaming and pale. It made the other buildings seem squalid and shrunken next to it. They were covered in posters with a man's face on them, and the words THORSEN FOR GOVERNOR. But there were no posters on the tower; its mysterious, Glory-days material shone like new.

The square was lit up with large spotlights and was busy. Men in black uniforms ran back and forth, carrying equipment and clipboards, and pots of food bubbled in one corner. Dogs barked and whined in cages. One building was lit up, with guards standing outside. There were more humans than Cora had ever seen in her life.

Seleen tapped her on the shoulder. "We should go," she whispered. As they crept away, she muttered, "I need to get into that office, work out where they've already searched. Then we can slip in behind them."

Cora asked, "What do we do now?"

They reached the end of the alley, past bins and scattered debris. A rat or some other small creature rustled behind the bins. In her normal voice, Seleen said, "We'll need somewhere here to stop until later. Down by the—"

Then there was a blur as Seleen lunged in between the bins, and a startled yelp. And suddenly Seleen was striding forward, pushing something ahead of her, and then she was lifting it against the wall, pinning it with one hand while the other pulled a knife from her belt as she snarled, "*What are you doing here?*"

The figure threw its arms up into the air.

"Please don't kill me!" it squeaked.

It was Kai.

"What are you doing here?" growled Seleen again, holding her knife to Kai's throat.

"Nothing!" gasped Kai.

"You were following us."

"No! I mean, kind of. But I was just trying to see what was happening! Please!"

"So what *is* happening?" demanded Seleen.

Kai swallowed. "The town's gone crazy. There are armed police everywhere, Protection troops. They're arresting anyone new in town – they were searching my place when I got back! They're looking for ... for..." He blinked. "I think they're looking for *you*."

Seleen grimaced and let him go, and he slumped to the ground.

"They're searching for a girl," he said, glancing up at Cora. "And someone else, really dangerous. Someone called Lilith?"

"Who's that?" asked Cora. "Seleen? Who's Lilith?"

Seleen ignored her. "Did they say where they've searched?"

Kai shook his head. "No."

Seleen nodded. "We still have to get their plans." She pointed her knife at Kai and he cringed. "We're going," she said. "*Don't* follow us. Come on, Cora."

"But where will you go?" he called. "They're everywhere!"

Cora said, "We'll hide in the woods."

97

"Cora," warned Seleen.

"You'll freeze to death!"

"We've got power cells, we'll be fine."

"*Cora!* Come *here!*"

Kai scratched his head. "But won't the Scanner find you?"

Seleen halted. "What do you mean?" she asked in a wary voice.

"The Cell Scanner," said Kai. "They've got it here with them."

Cora asked, "What's a Cell Scanner?" Seleen was frowning as if she'd already guessed and didn't like the answer.

Kai looked between them. "Well … it, uh, scans. For cells. All the new cells have got tracking devices, you know? When you use the cells, the Scanner can track them. Like, from kilometres away. It's some new Glory technology; they discovered it a couple of years ago. I heard they've got it here in Recon."

Cora remembered the strange device the soldiers had been setting up outside the cabin. She turned to Seleen, but Seleen was already nodding. "That's why they made everyone get new cells," she muttered, glaring into the distance. "That's how they found us."

She thought for a moment, and then nodded. "Come

on, Cora, we have to go."

"Take me with you?" asked Kai. "I could help!"

"No," said Seleen.

"You're going to Base, aren't you?" he asked. Seleen stiffened, and glared at him, but he plunged on. "Or Sheen. That's your new plan, isn't it? I mean, you have to, right? You want to stay off-grid, but you can't survive the winter without power. You *need* power cells, ones without trackers. And I bet someone like you could get hold of them – *if* you can make it to Base."

Seleen said nothing, and Kai nodded. "Well, I can get you there, real quick."

"How?" asked Cora.

Kai shook his head. "Take me with you."

"I could kill you right now," Seleen muttered.

But he seemed more confident now. "Then you won't know."

"I could wait till you tell me, and *then* kill you," she said.

"She's kidding," said Cora hurriedly. Seleen raised an eyebrow.

Kai sighed. "Look: you need to get to Base, I want to avoid Sisal's troops. We help each other, make it out, split, and you'll never see me again. Come *on*."

Cora bit her lip. "Maybe we should," she said to Seleen. "He knew about the Scanner. He might be able to help.

And besides…" She looked at him. "If Sisal's as bad as you say, we can't just *leave* him here. He's hopeless."

Kai nodded desperately. "It's true, I am! I really am."

Seleen scowled at him for a long time. But at last she nodded.

"As far as Base."

"Great!" cheered Kai. He grinned. "You're gonna *love* this."

Escape

It was still dark. Sisal's Protection troops were in the square, but local police guarded the rest of the town, and Seleen slipped past them like smoke, leading Cora and Kai out of Recon before dawn. Then they followed Kai up into a forest to the south, hiking another kilometre under snow-covered trees, until they reached a clearing covered in dead brushwood.

"Here," said Kai. He shifted the branches aside to reveal a glint of grey battered metal, which became a strange, flat device. It was like a platform, three metres long and two wide, but only a quarter-metre thick, with a thin rail around the edges and some sort of controls at one end. It seemed ancient; every surface was scraped, and black soot marks spread up the sides.

Seleen examined it. "This is yours?" she asked. Cora thought she sounded grudgingly impressed.

He nodded. "Sure."

"Looks pretty smashed."

Kai shook his head. "It's fine. It brought me all the way from Base. It just needs power."

"Hmm. And you ... *found* this?" asked Seleen.

"Yes." Kai looked at her levelly. "You're not the only one who's good at finding things."

She met his gaze for a moment or two and Cora thought she almost smiled. Instead, she sniffed. "Well, let's get going then."

"What is this?" asked Cora.

"Transport," said Seleen. She pulled their power cells from her bag, and Kai opened a flap on the side of the machine to reveal a wide slot.

"These cells are tracked, remember," he warned. "Once we activate them, Sisal's troops will be able to scan us." Seleen nodded, and carefully slid the cells in.

Lights blinked on the controls and they made a chirping noise. Then the platform trembled and rose into the air.

Cora yelped and leapt backwards. "What's it *doing*?" she gasped. It lifted until it was a half-metre off the ground and stopped, perfectly still.

"Pretty cool, eh?" said Kai. He stepped up on to the platform. It didn't move under his weight. Grinning, he turned and reached a hand towards Cora.

"Would you like to join me?" he asked grandly.

Cora peered underneath. "How is it *doing* that?" she asked. "What's holding it up?"

"I dunno," said Kai cheerfully. "No one knows. The Glories, right? Come on."

Cautiously, Cora climbed on to it. It stayed steady beneath her, as if rooted to the ground. The controls showed green lights and a screen with what appeared to be buttons with arrows. Beside her, Seleen stepped up without commenting.

"It's for cargo, really," said Kai. "But I added some straps. You should probably sit down and hold on to them. OK, I'm going to start slowly…"

He pressed a button and the platform slid forward. Cora grabbed a strap.

"It's OK, I'm OK!" she squeaked. The ground moved beneath them – no, it was the *platform* moving, floating over the ground towards trees at the edge of the clearing.

Seleen said, "Trees ahead."

"I'm on it," muttered Kai.

"Trees," she said again.

"Yeah, hang on. I think this— Wait, no-no-no—" The platform accelerated sharply, pulling them all backwards.

"*TREES!*"

"Yes!" Kai frantically pressed buttons. The trees rushed

103

towards them, suddenly very close and tall, and covered in sharp branches. Cora threw her hands up—

—And the platform lifted sharply and stopped, hanging in the air.

"Sorry about that!" chattered Kai. "Been a while, forgot the controls. Got it now."

Carefully, holding tight to the straps, Cora peered over the edge. They were ten metres off the ground, looking down at the treetops pointing up at them. The air was quiet, apart from a strange buzzing from one corner of the machine.

Kai tapped at the controls and the platform slid forward again, at walking pace. He turned a dial on the screen and it accelerated to a run. Then again, and again, and suddenly the forest below Cora was racing past.

The air was completely still, and there was a strange blurry edge all around them. Cora realised they were inside a bubble, extending a half-metre beyond the sides of the platform and a metre or two above. Distantly, through the blur, she could see Recon.

"Won't they be able to see us?" she asked.

Seleen nodded. "And scan us too. Can this thing go any faster?"

Faster? Cora closed her eyes as she felt again that push, like going downhill on a sledge. When she opened her eyes again the trees were moving too fast to make out.

"Oh, Glory," she muttered.

"We must be doing nearly two hundred kilometres an hour!" shouted Kai, delighted.

"Two hundred and three," muttered Cora automatically, watching the ground flick past.

Kai grinned. "They've got nothing that can go at that speed!"

Seleen said, "What's that noise?"

The buzzing was louder. "I don't know," said Kai. "It was like that when I found it. Seems to fly OK though."

Seleen frowned. "How long to Base?"

Kai studied the display. "It's about fifteen hundred kilometres, so—"

"Seven hours twenty-three minutes," said Cora. Thinking in numbers made it seem easier to cope with.

"And how wide is the scanning range?"

"About thirty K, I think," said Kai.

Seleen looked at Cora.

"Eight-point-eight-six minutes," said Cora. Kai blinked, but Seleen said nothing. Cora gazed around. Now that they'd reached top speed the pushing feeling had stopped. It was as if they were sitting still while the world itself raced past them. It was like magic. It *was* magic. Tentatively, she let go of one strap and reached towards the edge of the bubble. The air rushed past her fingertips, icy, like a fast-moving stream. She shivered.

They flew on, away from Recon and the mountain and over the course of a river that Kai said eventually led to Base. In a flicker, they travelled a distance that was an hour's walk. It was like stepping over a map. Was this what it had been like to be the Glories? Had they felt like giants all the time?

After a while, Seleen said, "We're out of scanning range now, yes?"

"I think so," said Kai. "We should be safe."

"Good. Turn and head for Sheen."

Kai frowned. "That wasn't the plan."

"It's the new plan," said Seleen. "If they're scanning us, they'll think we've gone to Base."

"I didn't agree to that."

"I didn't ask."

Kai glowered and folded his arms. "Without me to pilot, I don't think you're going anywhere," he declared.

Seleen gazed at him. "It doesn't look too hard. If there was an accident and you fell off, we'd probably be fine."

"*Seleen!*" gasped Cora.

Kai paled and tapped on the controls. "You know, you could have just *asked*," he grumbled. Cora felt the push again as the platform swung to its new direction. "If it

106

wasn't for me, you'd be caught by now."

"We'd be fine."

"Yeah, right," sneered Kai. "You think Sisal was here for a holiday? They were closing in on you."

Seleen said nothing.

"Who's Lilith?" asked Cora suddenly. Seleen looked surprised, and her face hardened as if she was going to ignore the question. Then she shrugged.

"Me," she said. "It's my name."

They were quiet for a while. Cora didn't quite know how to process this. Somehow, of all the surprises of the past twenty-four hours, this seemed the most shocking. *It's my name.*

Kai said, staring ahead to the skyline, "That's the wrong question anyway."

"What do you mean?" asked Cora. He shrugged.

"Look!" he said, pointing. "It's Outlook."

Up ahead stood an old tower, like the one at the centre of Recon; a Glory-days creation. But this one was burnt out, just a blackened shell with no roof.

"There's nothing there," said Kai. "I looked before. Creepy, eh? I heard that the ghosts of the Glories walk around there some nights." He laughed, slightly too quickly. "It's rubbish, of course."

Cora peered down at it. Glory buildings were shining

107

and indestructible. The sight of this ruined hulk was unsettling.

"Why did they leave?" she asked. "The Glories, I mean. Why did they leave us?"

Kai gazed at the tower. When he answered, he sounded unusually serious.

"We don't know what happened. It was about two hundred years ago, and there are only scraps of records. There's nothing to explain it. It's just, one day the humans woke up … and the Glories were gone. I mean, no one could even *remember* them, not properly. They'd left all their machines, but we didn't know how to use them. We didn't know they *were* machines at first. No one could make fire, or find food, even. It was pretty horrible, I guess."

Cora shook her head. "But why?"

"It doesn't matter," said Seleen. "They were then, and this is now. It's pointless to speculate."

Kai blew a sigh through his lips. "You're a whole bunch of fun, you know that?"

They flew on in silence, leaving the ruined building behind. The countryside was snowy and clean and empty of humans. Small herds of deer roamed unafraid on the hillsides below them, and birds flew close by.

Seleen made Kai show them how to work the controls,

and they took turns. It was simple enough: one dial for the speed, a sliding control for height – altitude, Kai called it – and a warning light that would show if anything needed doing. Cora took the first shift, then Seleen.

Kai and Cora stretched out on the platform while Seleen sat at the front. The thin rail around them seemed too frail to stop them rolling off, but as soon as she lay down Cora felt overwhelmed by a wave of tiredness she couldn't hold back.

Just before she succumbed, she remembered Kai's comment. "Kai?"

"Mmmm?"

"What was the question I should have asked?"

Kai, lying next to her with his arms behind his head, looked at Seleen's back.

"It's not about who she is," he murmured. "Cora… Who are *you*?"

The question followed her into sleep.

Lilith

Cora awoke from a dream of bees buzzing angrily around her head. She opened her eyes but the buzzing continued, coming from the back corner of the platform. Kai and Seleen sat at the front, frowning at the controls.

"That noise is louder than before," said Cora.

Seleen nodded. "We're running diagnostics now."

Cora came forward and looked at the panel. It was covered in strange writing, which moved up and disappeared off the top. New writing appeared from the bottom.

"What's diagnostics?" she asked.

"A tool to find out what's wrong," said Kai.

"What does it mean?"

Kai shrugged. The writing was a jumbling stream of letters, numbers and symbols, and seemed completely random. And yet, as Cora gazed at it, she had a strange feeling of recognition – as if she almost knew what it meant. And a hazy vision of that face again, the woman trying to tell her something, a warning…

"We have to land," she said suddenly.

The others looked at her in surprise. "It's just noise," said Kai. "She's still flying fine."

But Seleen glanced at Cora's face and frowned. "How far is it to Sheen?" she asked.

Kai pointed forwards. "See the mountain?" There was a tall, white-capped mountain about fifty kilometres ahead. "The hill in front of it is Sheen."

Cora peered at it. The hill seemed very steep, and it glinted in the pale morning sunlight. Metallic buildings sat all the way up its side.

"That's too far," she said. "We have to land *now*." She couldn't explain why, but she was certain.

"Find a landing place," said Seleen.

"But it's *fine*," said Kai, shaking his head. "Look, we've only got fifty—"

The platform *lurched*.

"Argh!" shouted Kai, as they grabbed straps. They dropped five metres and then levelled off. A large red symbol flashed on the display and the machine gave an angry squawk.

"What's happening?" demanded Seleen.

"I don't know!" wailed Kai.

"Go down *now*."

Kai tapped the screen. "Going down isn't a problem," he muttered. "Hang on."

The pallet fell again in a swoop that brought Cora's stomach up into her mouth. They were still hurtling along at top speed above the wooded hillside, but the trees seemed far too close, long branches flicking past them like spears.

"Slow down!" she shouted. Kai tapped the screen but nothing happened. The rattling sound grew louder, and suddenly the back-left corner dropped. Now the platform was leaning at an angle, threatening to tip them off.

Cora risked a glance ahead. "There!" She pointed. "There's a clearing!"

Kai nodded. "I see it!" He tapped, and the platform staggered downwards.

Seleen shook her head. "You're going too far left!"

"It's not steering properly!"

The back-left corner dragged them in the airstream like a rudder, ignoring Kai's attempts to control it. There was another stomach-flipping drop and a treetop whipped against them, shredding pine needles against the air bubble.

Cora stared at the panel, still scrolling its chaotic

messages, and blinked.

"I know what to do!" she shouted. She pushed past Kai, turned one dial to zero and slid a control to the side. The platform slowed and angled sharply back towards the clearing, and Cora felt a huge invisible force pushing her, threatening to shake her hand from the strap. The grass hurtled up at them and Kai scrambled backwards, and the display gave a harsh wailing *beeeep*—

They *smashed* into the ground. In a weird moment of clarity Cora saw the grass bending ahead of them, as the invisible air shield absorbed the first impact, slowing their collision. The platform dug into the earth and tipped forward until they were almost standing up on end, teetering … then collapsed back again on to its base with a bone-jarring crash. The wailing beep abruptly stopped.

There was silence.

Seleen stood up. "Everyone OK?" she asked. Kai and Cora, lying strewn on the remains of the platform, stared up at her. Seleen crouched next to Cora.

"Cora," she said. Her voice softened a little. "Look at me. Can you focus?"

Cora blinked a few times until the different versions of Seleen's face settled into one. "Yes," she muttered.

Seleen examined her for a moment longer, then nodded, stood again and stepped off. "Come on, we have

113

to cover this up." She strode to the trees at the edge of the clearing and began cutting down branches.

Kai rubbed his face with shaking hands. "I'm fine too, by the way," he grumbled. He stared at Seleen, already dragging branches back to the platform as if nothing had happened.

"Is she always like this?" he asked.

"Always," sighed Cora.

They'd been lucky. The air shield had protected them from the worst of the crash, and no one was hurt, just scrapes and bruises and a ringing in Cora's ears that faded after a while. But they were still several kilometres from Sheen, and the platform would never fly again – its base had twisted when it hit the ground and the screen was cracked and frozen.

"How did you know what to do?" asked Kai.

Cora shrugged and ducked her head. "I don't know. Lucky guess."

"But you knew it was going to crash too."

Cora remembered the image of the woman, appearing as the diagnostic messages had scrolled past. It was as if she'd been warning her. As if she'd known…

Seleen thrust an armful of branches at Kai. "She's a quick learner," she said. "Stop talking and help with this."

Kai seemed about to argue, but shrugged. "Whatever you say."

They covered the flyer, and the tracks scarred into the earth by their landing. The camouflage wouldn't stand up to proper inspection, but it might make it less obvious from a distance. Kai stared at the wreckage with a sad expression.

"I loved that thing," he said.

"I bet its real owner did too," said Seleen. "Time to move."

They headed away and into a thick forest. Just before the trees obscured it, Cora caught sight of the city of Sheen, shining against the mountain behind it.

It made no sense. The hill it sat on seemed ridiculously steep, almost vertical. She could make out buildings and farms spreading out from the bottom, but they seemed tiny, and there were strange round black structures at the base.

"Why did they build on the hill?" she asked. "Why not by the river?"

Kai grinned. "You'll see."

They hiked down through the forest for several hours until they reached the plains. The trees thinned out and now, less than a kilometre away, Cora saw Sheen at last.

She looked up at it. And up, and up. And then down, to the enormous base and the vast black shapes at the bottom. She could see what they were now.

They were *wheels*.

She looked up again at the sides, full of windows and portholes glinting in the pale sunlight. Her mouth fell open.

"Welcome to Sheen," said Kai.

"What *is* it?" she managed. It was too big. It loomed over her, somehow seeming taller even than the mountain. It couldn't be a made thing. Nobody could make that. The wheels were larger than the tower back in Recon. How could it have *wheels*?

Kai said, "The Glories built it."

"Come on," snapped Seleen, striding ahead of them. Cora stumbled after her. Wheels…

"But … does it move?"

"Not now. But in Glory times, yes. It's a machine." Kai grinned again.

"But then … then…" The size of it pushed everything else out of Cora's head. She tried again. "If it's a machine, then what was it for?"

Seleen blew out a breath of exasperation. "Hurry *up*," she called over her shoulder.

"We don't know," said Kai. "But we think it was eating the mountain."

The answer made so little sense that Cora couldn't

think how to respond.

Before they reached the buildings, Seleen led them on a detour into a steep hollow, hidden from sight. She scanned a mound of ancient rubble, then headed towards a boulder marked with red lichen, and cleared away some grass from it. She reached into a gap and pulled out an old bag.

"You've been here before then?" asked Kai.

"A while ago," she said. "Left some stuff." She opened the bag and retrieved a battered red leather jacket and jeans, and changed into them. Kai blushed and turned around until she was done.

The jeans were a little tight, and Seleen cursed as she fastened them. "Fat and old," she muttered. Then thick-soled boots, and the jacket, which seemed to have metal plates sewn into it. Then a small crossbow; she attached the cord and tested it with her thumb, frowning, before placing it in a holster behind her back. Then a few other devices packed into pockets, and a bundle of credits. She used a piece of rawhide to tie her hair, and shoved her old clothes into the gap.

Then she stood and looked at Cora.

Cora stepped back. Seleen could be stern, scary even, but this creature was something else. Her face and body language were different, somehow. She loomed over

Cora, blood-red, poised and dangerous.

"My name is Lilith," the creature said.

Cora stared.

"Your parents asked me to protect you. People are looking for you. We have to make sure they never find you. That's all that matters."

This strange new person – this *Lilith* – turned and pointed at the massive structure. "We're going into Sheen so I can find a way for us to hide again. You've never been to a place like this. You will do what I tell you. Understand?"

Cora blinked and nodded.

"Good. Follow me."

The woman who had been Seleen walked away. Behind her, Cora looked at the pile of old clothing discarded under the boulder. Then she followed Lilith out of the hollow.

Lilith led them to the end of the vast edifice – Cora still struggled to think of it as a machine – past small farmsteads and houses. It wasn't like walking into Recon. There it had been night-time, and the only ones around had been the soldiers in the square. Here there were *people*, dozens of them. They didn't seem interested in these strangers; hardly paid them any attention at all. Occasionally, one of them seemed amused at Cora, who was staring open-mouthed at everything.

Lilith stepped on to a ramp leading up to the entrance.

"Watch your possessions," she muttered. The ramp was lined with market stalls, and hundreds of people bustled around them, more than Cora had ever seen, buying and selling, calling from their stands, speaking over her to each other, bumping into her, shouting and gesticulating. Pans of food sizzled and simmered with smells that made her head swim with hunger. Everyone wore winter coats, and steam rose from their mouths and the cooking pots.

It was overwhelming. Beside her, Kai strolled along, seeming to slip through the crowd without thinking, while Cora blundered and stumbled and apologised. How was he doing it? The sheer number of people overwhelmed her, and she crashed into a stall selling coats. The stall-owner shouted something at her. Cora blinked at him, startled, until Lilith came back.

"It was an accident," Lilith said to the man.

"She spilled paint on this, look!" he complained.

"No," said Lilith, smiling with just her teeth. "She didn't."

Kai wormed Cora away while Lilith handled things. "It's OK," he said. "Don't expect it to make sense, just relax and keep moving."

Cora stared at him. "It's *chaos*!" she whimpered.

"No, no," he laughed. "It's just people. We're almost there. Deep breaths, OK?"

Lilith caught up with them. "Stay with me," she muttered, and forged ahead.

They were nearly at the top of the ramp now, ten metres or more above the ground. There were guards at the entrance, and barriers, and a woman sitting inside a booth. When people wanted to enter, they had to show her cards with writing on them.

"ID cards," murmured Kai.

Cora didn't have a card. Did she need one? Had Seleen thought of that?

Lilith, she corrected herself. *Not Seleen*.

"Give me yours," Lilith muttered, and Kai handed his over. She strode to the booth, nodded to the woman and passed the card across, with something tucked next to it.

The woman suddenly seemed to lose all interest in them. She returned the card but not the other thing, gazed off into the distance and pressed a button on her desk. The barrier next to the booth unlocked, and Lilith gestured them through.

"What just happened?" whispered Cora as they entered.

"Money," said Lilith. "Welcome to Sheen."

Sheen

It was darker inside, and it took a few seconds for Cora's eyes to adjust from the sharp winter sunlight. Then she realised she was in a hall larger than any building she'd ever known. It towered above her to a ceiling supported by massive steel arches. The walls were a hundred metres away in every direction.

It was a marketplace. The stalls from the ramp spread inside and covered the entire floor, hundreds of them, laden with food, clothes, equipment, toys, religious items, Glory technology... Everything Cora could imagine, and much that she couldn't. Huge steel ridges stuck out from the walls like honeycombs, forming metal caves with more shops and bars built into them. It was hot and noisy and humid.

And there were *thousands* of people. They slid and bumped and jostled past Cora, tall and thin and short and fat, old and young, loud and quiet, filling the space with conversations and arguments and laughter, wearing strange clothes Cora had never seen before – long drapes and tall hats, shoes with high heels, brightly coloured or deep black, every outfit different from the one before.

Lilith ignored them all. She led the others towards the left wall, cutting through sellers and buyers, and Cora concentrated on keeping up before the crowd closed in like water behind her.

"Stop!" she called at last. "Seleen, stop! Where are we going?"

"Up," Lilith growled. "And you may as well call me Lilith now."

She entered a metal cage and gestured impatiently for the others to follow, then she closed the front gate and pressed a button at one side. To Cora's alarm the cage shuddered and then lurched upwards, and she grabbed at a handrail.

"It's a lift," said Lilith. "Nothing to worry about."

Suddenly Cora was angry. "I'm not worried!" she snapped. "*Lilith*."

They stood in silence as the cage rose.

"So," said Kai brightly. "What's the plan?"

"New IDs first," said Lilith. "And then power cells. Untraceable cells, without trackers, so we can hide somewhere through the winter without their Scanner finding us. I have some old friends here who might help me out."

She nodded to Kai. "I'll sort a new ID for you, too. And some money, and transport to Base."

Kai shrugged. "Money and ID is enough. I've got my own route back."

The cage stopped with a jerk, and Lilith hauled the door open. "This way." She led them along a balcony, glanced round, then slipped into a recess between two pipes. There was a panel on the wall, and Lilith removed it and peered inside.

"In here."

They climbed into a small storage room with boxes piled up against one side.

Lilith said, "I need to talk to some people. You stay here."

Cora turned. "What?"

"I'll be back soon."

"Why can't we come with you?"

Lilith grimaced. "It might be a loud conversation. I might have to move quickly."

"We slow her down," said Kai cheerfully. He sat on a box. "Got any food?"

Lilith nodded. "In the rucksack." She left, putting the

panel back up after her. Cora contemplated the panel for a while and then sat down.

"Cargo," she muttered.

Kai looked up. "What is?"

"Me."

Call me Lilith now. Cargo. Something put into storage. Cora glowered and reached into the bag for a strip of jerky, and chewed at it while they waited.

It was over an hour before Lilith returned, and by the time she opened the panel, Kai was wondering out loud where there might be some toilets.

She stood at a slight angle, as if stiff. "IDs," she muttered, holding up two cards.

There was something that looked like blood on her glove.

Kai carefully picked a card out of her hand, and after a moment so did Cora. *Malenka du Pris*, it read.

"We still need power cells," said Lilith. "I heard there's a dealer on top deck who has some. I'll try her next."

"I'm coming with you," said Cora.

"No."

"Why not?"

Lilith stretched, winced and rubbed her shoulder. "Sheen's a rough place. The people I'm meeting are unpredictable. It's safe here."

"It was safe in the cabin – until it wasn't." Cora stood and faced Lilith. "I'm not a bag you can just leave somewhere. I'm coming with you."

"Also, I *really* need the toilet," said Kai.

"What do you think this is, a picnic?" snapped Lilith. She rubbed her forehead. "Fine. Might be better to stay together anyway. But when we reach top deck you wait outside, no arguing, understand?"

Cora nodded.

"Come on then."

She picked up a rucksack and climbed out through the gap, Cora and Kai scrambling after her. Lilith didn't wait for them but strode towards the cage and pressed the button, making them run to reach it before the doors closed.

The lift juddered upwards, and the hall was soon far below them. Cora stared down. The people in the markets, as tiny as insects from her viewpoint, gave the place its scale. It was as big as Recon – but Recon was a whole town. This was just one room, and it was *huge*.

"What's it *for*?" Cora asked.

"What do you mean?" asked Kai.

The cage stopped and they came out on to a balcony near the top. Cora waved her hand down at the massive hall. "Why build something this big?"

Lilith shrugged. "Who cares?" But Cora obstinately stopped and leaned against the rail, looking down. The view was dizzying.

Kai said, "See the solid buildings? The Glory-made ones?"

Cora nodded. They were scattered in between the stalls, squat black columns a few metres tall.

"There used to be a track that sat on them, and machines all around them, grinding, like teeth. The Glories carved off bits of the mountain and put them on to the tracks, and then the machines ate them."

"Fascinating," said Lilith. "Move."

"Who are they?" asked Cora. She pointed down at more figures entering the hall. They were different, she could tell even from here. They wore black uniforms and they moved in an organised pattern.

Lilith frowned. "Protection troops," she muttered.

"There are some on the lower balconies too," said Kai. "Look."

Cora's mouth had gone dry. "Are they here for us?" she asked.

Lilith checked their floor. "They can't be. It'll be hours before anyone could get here from Recon without a flyer, and it's too far for their radios."

"Um…" Kai frowned. "What about the Long Wave?"

"The what?"

"You know, their radio thing, only for really long distances. Couldn't they use that?"

Lilith stared at him. "I don't—" she started. "I didn't know about that. They can do that? Why didn't you tell me?"

"How could you *not* know that?" exclaimed Kai. "They showed it at the Glory Day celebration!"

Lilith grabbed the front of Kai's shirt. "What else?" she demanded. "Cell trackers, long-distance radio… What else have they got now?"

"I don't know!" he spluttered. "I mean, they find new technology all the time—"

But Lilith wasn't listening. "I've been gone too long," she muttered. "I'm a *fossil*." She shook her head. "That means they know we could be here. They'll check the entrance, the guard will remember us, they'll start locking down. We need a way out."

She strode along the balcony. "Follow me," she commanded. "Don't run, don't look at them. This way." Cora and Kai stumbled after her. The urge to look was almost overwhelming. Cora was certain there was someone behind her, closing in; a black-gloved hand was about to grab her shoulder, a voice would shout out—

"Here." Lilith stopped at what looked like a service hatch, and opened it. "In."

Inside there was a small metal platform and a ladder. Lilith closed the hatch behind them and stepped on to the ladder.

"Don't get too close," she said. "And no talking from now on." She started climbing down, with Cora after her and Kai last.

They climbed and climbed. Cora was used to mountain hiking, but the movement was unusual and her legs soon ached. Each floor was thirty steps high. How many floors had there been? Twenty, she thought. Six hundred steps in total. Above her, she heard Kai's laboured breathing; below, Lilith's steady, clumping steps.

Three hundred steps. Kai cursed as his foot slipped, and he skidded down two metres before catching himself with a jolt. The ladder twanged and Cora cringed below him, but nothing else happened. He clung on, panting. Lilith paused, then continued climbing down. Occasionally sounds echoed through the wall; conversations, shouting. Cora concentrated on the steps. Five hundred now. Her hands were slick with sweat, and Kai was panting with every step, rasping breaths like sobs.

Five hundred and fifty.

A louder noise now, and she realised in exhausted relief

that they had reached the market on the first floor. But Lilith kept going, to somewhere below the marketplace. Cora's legs were on fire, and her arms trembled. She couldn't hold on. She couldn't hold on…

"I can't hold on!" gasped Kai above her. He sounded panicky.

"Quiet!" hissed Lilith. "We're almost there."

"But I can't hold *on*."

Lilith was speeding up. Cora tried to hurry but her feet wouldn't cooperate. She stumbled, and then there was a clattering sound above her and a shout from Kai, and he crashed down on to her.

"Argh!"

She tried to hang on, but her hands were lumps of meat, unable to follow instructions any more. Cora and Kai fell together, the rungs battering Cora's arms as she tried desperately to regain a handhold. They collided with Lilith, who gave a startled grunt. She couldn't take the weight of them both and they barrelled down the ladder—

And hit the ground, two metres below, Lilith first, then Cora, then Kai on top of them both, sprawling into an ungainly heap on the floor.

Lilith cursed and pushed them away, and then froze. Cora looked up. A man in a blue guard's uniform had come round the corner and was staring at them in astonishment. He was holding a gun but it wasn't raised. He was only two metres away.

"What the—"

Lilith lunged towards him, but her feet slipped against the metal decking, just for a moment. It was enough for the man to bring his gun up and fire two shots.

Lilith jerked and fell to the floor.

"*Seleen!*" screamed Cora.

The man raised his gun again. "Stay where you are!" he shouted, but Cora ignored him and ran to Lilith, lying still on the deck. She rolled her over and an arm flopped down. One bullet had hit Lilith's chest, the other her neck. There was blood everywhere. Her eyes were open but unblinking.

She was dead.

Base

"Lilith!" wailed Cora. "Lilith, wake up!" Lilith's eyes stared back at her, glassy and empty. Dead. "Seleen!"

"Put your hands up!" shouted the guard.

Cora ignored him. In her mind she saw the bullets again, hitting Lilith once, twice. *Seleen!* Almost without trying, she *looked* and could see the causes, the thousand tiny threads and paths that led to Lilith's death. The bullets hitting. The trigger pulled. The guard, surprised as he came around the corner, the fall, the ladder slick under her hands—

"I said, put your hands up! On your head!"

The gun. The trigger pulled, and within the gun's chamber a metal spike smashing against the base of the bullet, creating an explosion, firing the bullet. Killing Seleen…

No.

131

And this was the other thing she could do.

She remembered Kai, back at the cabin, talking about her power. *Does it work with people?* he'd asked. Cora had been horrified.

No.

The fall, the bullet wound, they were too large to change. Something small. She closed her eyes, watched the spike against the bullet, and with all her will she imagined something different – the base resisting, bending but not breaking, not creating the spark it needed to fire—

The butt of the guard's gun crashed into her back.

"HANDS ON YOUR HEAD!" he shouted. Cora sprawled over Lilith's corpse.

No.

It was too hard. The hammer was too heavy, pain pulsed red above her eyes, it was too *hard*… And then it changed. In her mind, she slowed the spike enough, just enough to cause the bullet to misfire. She *fixed* that point, and felt events reflow around her, around all of them…

Time changed.

Lilith lunged towards the guard just like before, and he fired, but now the gun just clicked. He pulled the trigger again, but Lilith was accelerating and his second shot was too low. She fired her crossbow as they collided; the crossbow bolt punched his shoulder and he dropped to the deck with Lilith on top.

Cora felt a warm, damp sensation on her lip and realised her nose was bleeding. She slumped into a faint. When she awoke, for a moment, she saw the woman's face again, floating in front of her, gazing at Cora with her expression of calm concern, saying something. Something important…

Seleen!

Cora opened her eyes. Seleen … *Lilith* was lying on the deck, Kai leaning over her. She was breathing hard and quick, her jacket and T-shirt ripped open. Kai was pressing a piece of her T-shirt against her side like a bandage. There was blood everywhere.

"Seleen!"

"It's OK!" shouted Kai. "She's alive!"

Lilith's face was screwed up in pain, but she was alive.

"Jacket took most of it," said Kai. "But she's lost blood. Bullet's inside, I think. The guard's unconscious."

Relief flooded through Cora like a wave. "I thought you were——"

With great effort, Lilith turned her head to Cora. "No. Come here."

Cora knelt beside her. Lilith was pale and sweating. "I was … dead," she said.

"Yes."

"You *fixed* me."

Cora smiled. "Yes."

Lilith nodded. Then one hand swung and slapped Cora's face, hard. "*Never do that! Never!*"

"What?" Cora recoiled in shock. Her face stung. "You were *dead*!"

"Doesn't *matter*!"

"Of course it matters! What's *wrong* with you?"

Lilith panted. "You need to run," she whispered. "Kai – you said you had a way to get to Base."

Kai frowned. "Yes."

"Take Cora."

The boy nodded.

"What are you talking about?" demanded Cora. "You have to come with us!"

"Go without me."

"No!" Cora was suddenly furious. "I *saved your life*! I'm not leaving you! You're so stupid!"

"Cora, I can't *move*."

"*Fine*." Cora crossed her arms. "I'll stay here with you."

Lilith's eyes closed, and she ground her teeth. "Help me up," she grunted at last.

Kai hesitated. "If the bullet's inside you, that's a really bad idea—"

"*Help. Me. Up.*"

"OK, OK!" He helped her into a sitting position. She shuddered.

"On to my feet," she hissed.

Together, Kai and Cora lifted her until she was leaning against the tunnel wall, panting. She glared at Cora.

"Thirteen years protecting you," she wheezed. "And you'd throw it away out of *sentiment*." She turned to Kai. "Where do we go?"

"Hospital."

"No, I mean to *escape*."

Kai nodded. "Trust me."

They stumbled through the deserted basement corridors, dragging Lilith between them as she sweated and groaned, until they reached a door with a large green cross.

"Around the corner," Kai murmured. They staggered round and lowered Lilith to the ground.

"I need to talk to someone," he said. "Give me all your money."

Lilith glowered at him suspiciously.

"Here," said Cora, fetching Lilith's purse and pulling out the credits. Kai tipped them a salute and left. They heard him knock on the door, in a pattern – *tap, pause, tap-tap*. Then a wait, then conversation – Kai cheery and joking, the other voice suspicious. Then the door closed and Kai was gone.

Cora sat with Lilith and waited for him to come back. Her cheek still hurt.

"Why did you do that?" she asked.

Lilith's eyes were closed, and Cora thought she might be asleep. But then she said, in a surprisingly clear voice, "You can't *ever* use your powers."

"I saved your life!"

Lilith grimaced. "What about the guard?"

"What?"

"The guard. You nearly killed him, you know."

Cora's mouth fell open. She realised she hadn't thought about the guard at all. He'd killed Lilith, and Cora had fixed it. Instead it had been Lilith who shot the guard, and then knocked him out.

"But I—"

"If you'd killed him, would you have brought *him* back? If it meant I died?"

"But that's—"

"Do you think he has a family?"

Cora recoiled. "What?"

"That's the first time," whispered Lilith. "And you'll say you had no choice, but you did. And you'll have a choice next time, and the time after that. And the things *you* can do… You *can't* use your powers, Cora. You're too

136

much…" She slumped.

"Lilith?"

"*Too much like me.*" She slid to the ground and her breath rattled out.

"Lilith!" Cora tried to lift her back up, but she was too heavy. Her eyes fluttered and closed. "Seleen!"

A shadow fell across them. "Out of the way!" Someone pulled at Cora. "I'm a doctor, move away!" A woman in a green outfit took Lilith's pulse and checked the wound. She nodded to another medic, and they heaved Lilith on to a stretcher and carried her away.

Cora stumbled after them and found Kai.

"It's OK!" he said, lifting his hands. "They're good guys. Good guys!"

He sniffed.

"Well… Not *cheap* guys, anyway."

"Cora." Kai tapped her shoulder. "Time to go."

Cora blinked. She'd been lying across three chairs in the waiting room, asleep. She rubbed her face.

"Is she…?"

Kai nodded. "She's OK. The bullet's out. Still unconscious. Come on."

The woman in the green outfit was waiting for them, with two orderlies and a trolley. Lilith lay on the trolley, unconscious, her face grey and slack. The orderlies pushed her out, and Cora and Kai followed them.

"Where are we going?" asked Cora.

Kai said, "Transport to Base."

"But won't Sisal's guards be waiting?"

Kai grinned. "Wait and see."

They followed the trolley to a loading bay and a single large black container, with yellow lettering that read: "DANGER! INFECTIOUS BIOMATTER DISPOSAL". The orderlies wheeled Lilith inside.

The doctor turned to Kai. "They'll move you off at the other end," she said. "She'll need these – here." She gave him three small silver sachets.

"Wow," said Kai, his eyes widening. "Thanks. I owe you one."

"Yeah, yeah. Go." She turned to Cora. "Good luck," she said. Cora noticed she wore a thin silver necklace with a pendant in the shape of a star.

"Come on," said Kai. Cora followed him into the container. There was a single lamp inside, enough to see discarded boxes and some bedding in a corner, and a couple of bottles of water. Lilith lay on a thin mattress on the floor.

Kai closed the door. "They'll pick us up soon."

"Who?"

"Oh, just people." He waved an arm vaguely. "They'll load us on to the transport. We should be fine. For some reason, the guards never want to search the carriage full of plague corpses."

Cora nodded. "What are those silver things?"

"Glory medicine – *very* rare. They stop pain and infection."

There was a clatter against the sides of the container, and the whole thing lifted in the air, swayed, and dropped back down with a crashing thump. Then a long wait, and finally an ominous rumbling sensation beneath them that started low and built up to a steady throb.

Kai blew out a breath. "Next stop, Base," he said. "It's about three hours. I'm going to get some sleep."

Cora nodded, but stayed next to Lilith, holding her hand as she listened to Kai's soft snoring. Her cheek no longer hurt where Lilith had slapped her, but it still felt warm.

Cora had saved Lilith's life. She'd used her powers for something *good*, something *important* – not just catching rabbits, or dice tricks, but something that really mattered. Surely that was right? What was the point of having extraordinary abilities if she didn't use them? *You nearly killed him*, she heard Lilith say again, but she shook her head. It made no sense. She sat, feeling the rumble of the wheels below her, and fell asleep.

When she awoke, Lilith's eyes were open. She was still lying on the mattress and seemed groggy.

"Where am I?" she asked in a scratchy voice.

"Transport," said Kai. He sat leaning against the side. "Inside a medical container. Some friends of mine use it to move stuff between Sheen and Base."

"Stuff?"

Kai shrugged. "Stuff they don't want to go through customs. Glory medical supplies the government doesn't want us ordinary mortals to have access to."

"Well, aren't you just full of surprises?" said Lilith.

He smiled. "I'm good at finding things." He handed her the silver packets. "Doc said you'd want these."

Lilith raised her eyebrows when she saw them. She pulled her sheet back and examined a long bandage wrapped around her middle. She sat up, wincing in pain.

"Anything to drink?" she asked. Cora silently handed her a bottle of water. "Thanks."

They didn't make eye contact. Lilith leaned against the wall and then worked her way up to standing, accompanied by muttered swearing. She opened one of the sachets and tipped a strange blue gel into her mouth, and after a few seconds her face relaxed.

"Don't overdo it," said Cora. "It could reopen."

Lilith nodded. The engine noise changed key.

"We're here," said Kai. "They'll unload us, and then we can leave." He examined Lilith. "What's your plan when we get there?"

Lilith didn't answer. Her face fixed into a hard expression, deliberately blank, and Kai sighed.

"*Fine*," he said crossly, and folded his arms. "If I'd wanted to hand you in I could have done it in Recon. You're only here now because of me, you can barely stand up, and I'm offering to help, but sure – you just carry on being all silent and dangerous. Good luck trying to walk out of here."

There was an awkward silence. Lilith grimaced and glanced at Cora.

"I know a place," she muttered finally. "You can come along, if you must."

Kai shrugged. "Well, maybe I will. Just for a bit." He smiled. "Since you asked so nicely."

After a while they heard the same clattering as before, and the familiar lift, swing and crashing drop. They waited a little longer and then slipped outside. They were in another loading bay, this one in the open air. It was dark, still before dawn, and soft lights glowed up ahead. The air was freezing and smelled of oil and stale food.

Lilith nodded. "Over there," she said. "Up the hill."

They crept out of the bay, Kai leading and Lilith limping behind. Lilith was sweating even in the cold. She made it as far as the fence, swallowed the contents of the second sachet and then somehow hauled herself over before collapsing with a groan.

Cora checked the bandages. "You've reopened the wound," she said.

"Not far," gasped Lilith. "Keep going."

Cora looked around. Base seemed like Recon, but with many more buildings – she could see dozens of houses, lines of them, neat and identical. The road was coated in a smooth black material she'd never seen before, and there were lights at the sides of the road every ten metres. Kai and Cora half carried Lilith up the hill. A light snow started falling, and the ground was slippery.

"Red door," Lilith gasped. Her head lolled forward.

One of the houses nearby did have a red door. Cora nodded to Kai, and they lurched towards it. Lilith was breathing in horrible retches, and her bandage was soaked red. Cora hesitated and then knocked. Nothing happened. She knocked again, louder, and after a few seconds they heard someone. The door opened a crack and a face peered out at them.

"What do you want?" it asked.

It was a woman's face, round and comfortable, topped

with a mass of brown hair wrapped in a net. It seemed like a kind face, though cautious.

"Sorry," gasped Cora. Lilith's dead weight was pulling her down. "Is this a – a safe place?"

"What?"

Kai said, "I think there's been a mistake."

"Well, I think so—" started the woman. Then she looked more closely.

"*Lilith?*"

"Do you know her?" exclaimed Cora.

"Lilith, is that *you*?"

Lilith pulled her head up and gave a grimace that might have been meant to be a smile.

"Hello, sis," she croaked.

Juliet

"Lilith!" the woman exclaimed. "What's happened?"

"Can we come inside?" gasped Cora.

The woman started. "Yes, yes, of course, come in!" She unlocked the door and opened it wide. "Oh, she's hurt! This way, this way! Oh, Lilith!"

She bustled down a narrow hallway and through a door on the left, and Kai and Cora followed her, dragging Lilith into a small room with a bed in one corner.

"Put her here," the woman said. "I'll get bandages. Oh, there's so much blood!" Her voice was raised in agitation, and her hands fluttered as she talked.

Lilith was nearly unconscious. She gasped, "*Blood on the path.*"

The woman looked blank. "Don't worry about that," she said. "We'll clean that up tomorrow, it's fine."

But Kai said, "She means we've left a trail."

"Oh." She stopped. "And that's… Someone's following you?"

"Yes," said Cora. There was no point in denying it.

"I'll sort the blood," said a voice.

Cora and Kai turned. In the doorway stood a teenage boy, a bit older than Cora. His face was like Lilith's, Cora thought, with the same hard features and jawline. He looked as if he'd just woken up; he was in a T-shirt and shorts, and his feet were bare. But he seemed alert.

He called over his shoulder. "Lotty! Get the first-aid kit!" He turned back. "How far back does the trail go?"

Kai looked at Cora, and she nodded. "Straight down the hill," Kai said. "To the loading bay. There's a fence – I think she started bleeding there."

The boy left, brushing past a small girl coming in with a bag and some towels. She stared at them open-mouthed.

"I brought…" she said, and hesitated.

Cora took the bag. "Thank you." It contained first-aid items – scissors, bandages, needle and thread. She examined them. Now what?

She realised she was waiting for Lilith to tell her what to do. But Lilith was unconscious now, her breath ragged. The large woman was leaning against the wall as if trying not to faint, and the girl seemed as startled as the rest of them. It was up to her, Cora realised.

What would Lilith do?

She stood up straight. "Kai, cut the old bandages," she said, handing him the scissors. "And then get that last sachet. It's in her jacket pocket."

She turned to the girl. "We need water," she said. "A bowl of boiling water, and another of very hot soapy water. Right now, go!" She tried to make her voice like Lilith's and it seemed to work – Kai and the girl jumped to follow her orders.

What next? Clean the wound, redo the stitches. There was thread in the bag, and a needle that looked sharp enough. Lilith had taught her how to do this; had made her practise with a dead deer one grisly afternoon. She could do it. The wound wasn't too bad, and still seemed clean.

Too much like me, Lilith had called her. *Well*, she thought, *let's see if that's true.*

Acting as if she knew what she was doing, Cora took off her coat and rolled up her sleeves. She picked up the needle and thread and tried to relax. The woman had found a chair and slumped into it, but the girl was wide awake and watching in fascinated horror. Partly to distract herself, Cora smiled at the girl.

"I'm Cora," she said. "And you're … Lotty?"

The girl nodded. She looked about ten, with long

hair in a braid; she held the end near her mouth and occasionally chewed on it.

"This is Kai," said Cora.

"Hey," said Kai.

Cora began stitching. Her hand was steady. She said, "This woman—"

"It's Auntie Lily," said Lotty.

Cora blinked. *Auntie Lily?*

"How do you know?"

"Mum's got a picture. She said no one's allowed to see it."

The woman stiffened. "That's enough, Lotty," she said. Her voice sounded a little firmer. She nodded to Cora. "I'm Juliet. Lily's my sister. Is she… Is she going to be all right?"

The last stitch went through, and Cora tightened and tied it off. "I think so. I'm not an expert, but she's pretty tough."

Juliet snorted and shook her head. "She is that."

The boy returned, now dressed and carrying a torch and a bucket of muddy red water. He stood in the doorway.

"I've cleaned the path," he said. "I wiped the fence too. Anything else?"

Cora nodded to the old bandages and bloody towels.

Her head felt suddenly heavy.

"That's my boy, Gavin," said Juliet. Cora nodded again. The room seemed dark and warm after the chill outside. She tried to stop her eyes from closing.

Juliet hauled herself to her feet. "Well," she said. "This story can keep till tomorrow. Lotty, we'll need beds for our guests."

"Yes, Mum."

Cora said, "I need to watch Lilith. Make sure the wound doesn't open again."

"I'll do that," Juliet reassured her. "You sleep. Lotty will show you where."

Cora wasn't sure she wanted to leave Lilith, but she was too tired to argue. As Lotty led them away, Juliet pulled her chair closer to the bed and sat down again.

"Ah, Lily," Cora heard Juliet mutter. "What trouble have you got yourself into now?"

Lotty led them to another small bedroom, with two beds covered in rumpled sheets.

"The bathroom is next door," she said shyly. "Do you need anything else?"

"No, thanks," said Kai, smiling. "This is great. Goodnight."

Cora ignored them and lay down. The bed was warm, and as soon as she closed her eyes, sleep overwhelmed her and she was gone.

She awoke to the smell of bacon cooking, and she lay still, letting her thoughts knit together, until she remembered the events of the previous day.

Lilith.

Cora sat up with a shock.

She was in a small room, alone. The room had a low ceiling, like their cabin, but painted white, the walls were covered in pale wallpaper with blue stripes, and there was a worn brown carpet on the floor. There were two beds, and the room was divided into neat halves; this must be where Lotty and the boy, Gavin, slept. An ancient toy fox lay at the end of her bed.

She heard sounds from next door: cooking, plates clattering, conversation. She crept into the hall, and then to the room where they'd put Lilith. Juliet's room, she thought. It was small; just a bed, a wardrobe and a dressing table, squeezed around each other. The bedspread was pink, and the dressing table was covered in a lace cloth embroidered with flowers. A dim light shone through cream curtains and lit up pictures hanging on the wall, drawn by children at various ages.

Lilith lay asleep in the bed, breathing calmly. Her face was grey and too thin, as if part of her had been burned up. Gingerly, Cora pulled back the blanket to examine the bandages. They seemed fine.

She looked around the room, and a painting caught her eye. It was a city, and the night sky above it. In the distance was Sheen, the enormous vertical town, and further still the tiny tower of Recon. Cora assumed the city was Base.

Above the city stood a woman. She stood as tall as the stars, and she seemed carved out of the midnight sky, with black-blue hair and dark robes pricked with dots of light. Her face was kind, and one arm reached out. Underneath the picture was a title: *The Lady Nostic protects us.*

"Morning," said a voice behind her. Cora turned.

Juliet stood in the doorway. In the morning light Cora could see a resemblance to Lilith; she was wider around the waist, more solid, but strong and tall, and her eyes had the same all-seeing sharpness.

"I guess Lily didn't mention me," she said with a wry smile.

Cora shook her head. "She doesn't say much about herself."

Juliet nodded. "She likes to keep us at arm's length. Reckons we're safer like that." She shrugged. "Maybe. She wouldn't have come here at all if she wasn't desperate."

"We're being hunted," said Cora. "We were attacked."

Juliet gave her a long, appraising look, and sniffed.

"You know what I think?"

"No?"

"I think no one's watching that bacon. *Lotty!* Bacon!" She nodded. "Come and get breakfast. Look at you, you're a rake. My sister ever feed you?"

She turned and left, and Cora, after a quick glance back at Lilith, followed her into a kitchen, thick with steam and noise and a smell of frying food that made her stomach growl. The kitchen was larger than the bedrooms, and floored with neat stone slabs that felt warm under her bare feet. Lotty stood at the stove, minding a huge pan of bacon and eggs. Behind her, Kai sat at a wooden table, eating heartily.

Juliet took over at the stove. "Our guest Cora here needs fattening up," she said to Lotty. She scooped bacon and eggs on to a plate, and Lotty brought it over with a quick shy smile. Cora sat next to Kai and smiled back at Lotty.

"Morning, lazybones," said Kai through a mouthful of food. Cora stuck her tongue out and then, unable to wait any longer, began devouring the bacon. Juliet brought the pan over again for Lotty, then herself, and for a while there was only the sound of contented munching. Juliet

151

poured thick coffee from a pot, and Cora ate and drank until she was stuffed.

The door clattered and Gavin came in, wearing a heavy winter coat that was covered in snow. He shut the door quickly behind him.

"Bad out there," he muttered.

Juliet frowned. "I've got to go shopping today," she grumbled, but the boy shrugged.

"Good for them," he said, nodding to Cora and Kai. "Any traces I missed will be covered until it thaws." His voice was gruff, and he looked stern. But Lotty laid out a plate for him and he smiled at her.

"So," said Juliet, at last, sitting back and wiping her mouth. "You want to tell me how you got here? And where my sister has been for the past thirteen years?"

Cora and Kai looked at each other. Cora said, "Lilith has been … looking after me. Keeping me hidden. But some people are looking for us, government people. And they found us, and we had to run, and she got hurt."

"Why are they looking for you?"

Cora bit her lip. "I don't know," she said. It wasn't a complete lie.

Juliet smiled. It was obvious she didn't believe Cora. She turned to Kai. "And what about you?"

Kai shrugged. "I'm her idiot friend," he said, jerking

a thumb at Cora. "I fell out of a tree and landed in the middle of this mess, I was just trying to get back to Base. I'll be off as soon as you stop feeding me bacon." He grinned, and Juliet and Lotty smiled back, charmed.

"Got some friends would like to meet you," said Gavin. "Anyone Thorsen wants, we want."

Juliet frowned. "Not now, Gavin."

"Thorsen?" asked Cora.

"Governor Thorsen, he means," explained Kai.

"It's not him looking for us," said Cora. "It's someone called Sisal."

Gavin leaned back in his chair. "Wow. You guys really *are* wanted. And you *escaped*?"

"Lotty, Gavin, it's time for school," said Juliet, cutting over him.

"If Sisal's after them they'll need protection—" Gavin started.

"By who?" snorted Juliet. "You and your *gang*? They *have* protection, the best kind – no one knows about them. And it stays like that, understand?"

Kai said, "If you're her sister, won't they check here?"

Juliet shook her head. "No one knows about us. Lily made sure of that a long time ago – we don't show up as related on any of their records. If she died, I wouldn't know a thing about it. Many times I've wondered if that's what had happened. If she'd died, and I just didn't know."

She blinked, stood, and gathered the dirty plates from the table. "No, you're safe if no one saw you arrive. Even if they did, we don't talk much to police round here. You stay, get better. You could use the rest, from the looks of you."

She clattered the plates into the sink and turned on the taps. "Thirteen years and not a word," she muttered. "I tell you, when that sister of mine is better I'm going to give her such a slap."

Recovery

Lilith was still asleep when Cora went to check on her, but she looked a little better. The grey pallor had retreated from her face and her breathing was even. Cora was about to leave when she opened her eyes.

She always woke instantly, Cora realised. Nothing in between, no drifting out of dreams. Was it a lifetime of danger, of being hunted? Would Cora become like that – always watchful, never relaxed?

Lilith glanced around the room. "Juliet," she muttered in a thick voice.

Cora nodded. "Last night, remember?"

"No." Lilith's brow creased. "I remember the fence. After that…"

"Your stitches tore. I restitched the wound."

Lilith nodded. "Is Juliet here?"

"Yes," said Juliet from the doorway. "Hello, sis."

Lilith looked up and grimaced. "Sorry for dropping in," she muttered.

"Dropping in is fine," said Juliet. "But if you try to leave again, I'll break your legs." She came over and checked Lilith's bandages. "Does it hurt? Itchy?"

"Not too much."

"Gavin can get more medicine. Not as good as that –" she gestured to the last silver Glory sachet, now empty "– but something."

Lotty and Gavin appeared at the doorway. "We're off to school, Mum," said Lotty. They gaped at Lilith.

"Auntie Lily and her friends are visiting for a bit, Lotty," said Juliet. "But it's a secret visit, understand? No telling your friends."

Lotty nodded, looking serious, and Juliet smiled at her. "Good girl."

Lilith said, "We should go. It's not safe for you." She tried to sit up, and winced. Juliet snorted.

"You wouldn't make it twenty metres. You'll stay and get better."

Lilith glowered, but didn't argue.

For the rest of the day Lilith drifted in and out of sleep, and Cora and Kai stayed inside. The little house was larger than Cora's cabin, but small for a family. Cora realised that they'd taken the bedrooms and everyone else had slept squeezed into one room at the front. Juliet insisted on it.

"You're our guests," she said. "It's no problem, we're snug as bugs."

That evening they sat at the kitchen table as Juliet served up bowls of stew. It was a loud, clattering meal, with Kai telling stories and Lotty chatting about school. Gavin didn't speak much. Occasionally he made some comment about politics, or his friends, but whenever he did, Juliet asked him loudly to pass the salt, or reminded him about something needing to be repaired.

Lilith slept through dinner. Later, Cora brought her a bowl of the stew.

"I like your sister," she said, feeding Lilith small spoonfuls.

"Don't be fooled," grunted Lilith. "When we were kids, she was a hair-puller."

"You named the goat Juliet."

"Yeah." Lilith gave an awkward cough. "Maybe don't mention that, eh?"

Cora nodded. "Lotty and Gavin seem nice too."

Lilith looked at her. "We can't stay here, you know."

"I know," said Cora, squirming. "I'm just saying,

they're nice."

"The longer we stay, the more danger there is for them. The plan's the same – find some untracked power cells and get far away."

"But isn't Base really big?" asked Cora. "Couldn't we hide here?"

"No."

Why not? thought Cora. But she suspected the answer would be "Because I say so".

Lilith finished her stew, and Cora inspected the wound. The stitches were holding, but the surrounding skin was raw and flushed. She frowned.

"We can't go anywhere until this settles down."

"We leave as soon as we can," said Lilith. "Understand? For their safety."

Cora nodded.

Lilith slept for long periods, and Cora sat by her bed and watched her.

She didn't know what to think about Lilith any longer. Juliet sent Lotty and Gavin to school, made sure they ate their vegetables, got them to brush their teeth and tidy up. Lilith had never done those things. Cora had never been to school – Lilith had taught her to read and write, and about the world (*but only what she wanted you to know,*

158

whispered a treacherous thought). Lilith had never told her to tidy – they were too busy setting traps, skinning animals, mending fences, and feeding the chickens or wringing their necks. Cora had assumed that was normal. Now, she wondered.

What am I to you? she silently asked Lilith. *What are you to me?*

On the second day, Kai physically dragged her away.

"Come *on*," he scolded. "Lilith's on the mend, she just needs time. Stop moping or I'll throw a bucket of water over you. Come and see this." He led her through the kitchen to the back door.

"We shouldn't go outside," warned Cora, but Kai snorted.

"The world is more than a big list of things you shouldn't do. Besides, who even knows we're in Base? Trust me." He opened the back door on to a small area surrounded by other houses. Washing lines hung empty and the world sat under a layer of snow. Cora could hear people, conversations, a hammering in the distance, but there was no birdsong, and no whistle of mountain wind. It had the same smell as Recon, that mix of wood smoke, cooking, rotted vegetation and many people living pressed up against each other.

"Here," said Kai, and led her up a ladder to a flat space

159

of roof. He swung his arm wide.

"*This*," he said, grandly, "is Base."

Cora had imagined something like Recon, a few dozen houses and farms surrounding a single tall building. But Base was *vast*. Where Sheen stretched tall, Base spread wide, as far as she could see – hundreds, *thousands* of buildings. Most were built low, with sloping roofs, but near the centre they grew taller, and some were three storeys high or more. And there were people everywhere, on every road, striding about on unknown business, talking to each other, buying and selling, pulling rickshaws.

"It's *enormous*," she gasped.

Kai grinned. "Isn't it great? I grew up over there – see Sanctuary? The orphanage is next to it."

He pointed towards a Glory building right in the centre. It was squat, spread out wide in front of the central square and topped with a dome. Its walls were an odd, dusty cream colour that made it look older than the others around it.

"What's Sanctuary?" asked Cora.

"It's like … Reverent headquarters," said Kai. "And a place for emergencies. All the buildings around it, they're government. But Sanctuary belongs to the church."

"So the Reverents are the church? And they're different to the government?"

Kai laughed. "Very different! Officially the government's in charge – they make the laws, they keep everything running. They're the brains, but the church is the heart. They ask awkward questions, kick up a fuss. They stand up for folk. People laugh at the Reverents, but they listen to them too. The government gives you order, but Sanctuary's where the first people went, after the Fall. Sanctuary gives you *hope*."

He beamed at the old squat building with a homeowner's pride.

The central square was covered in scaffolding and clambering workers. "What's going on there?" asked Cora.

"Preparations for Glory Day – big celebration, they hold it every year. Lots of parties, food, music, dancing. You'll love it."

"We won't be here for long," said Cora. "Lilith wants to move on."

Kai looked disappointed. "Well, at least let me show you around, yeah? Show you Sanctuary before you go?"

Cora shrugged. "Sure. Once Lilith is a bit better."

He smiled. "Good plan."

"We need power cells," said Lilith.

It was later that day. Lilith was sitting up in bed, and

Gavin was home from school. Lilith could barely move, but she was dismantling and cleaning her compact crossbow. Gavin watched.

"You can't get them," he said. "Not without trackers. I heard there's a warehouse in South where they've stored a few, just emergency stock, but the security's impossible. *Glory* tech." He frowned. "I'll ask if anyone knows a dealer. I know some folk."

Lilith nodded. "Thanks."

Gavin hesitated and then said, "Heard you were pretty good, in the day."

Lilith raised an eyebrow at him. "'In the day'? How old do you think I am?"

He shrugged. "Just, you know, stories Mum told us. Mad stories, like, killer robots and stuff." He laughed, and Lilith shrugged. Sunlight caught against the scar along her head.

"We could use that," said Gavin. "This place is a prison."

Lilith looked around the room. "Seems pretty nice to me."

"Not here. Out *there*. Protection troops are everywhere these days, clamping down. You can't do stuff, say stuff…"

"Not my problem," said Lilith. "It's a democracy; people vote. They voted for Governor Thorsen; they

162

knew all about Sisal."

"Yeah, but it's not *fair*," he complained. "The government's corrupt. Thorsen controls the news, Sisal doesn't let folk *speak*. They're taking more power, and we can't stop them. But you… Mum told me about some of the things you did. The underground hospital, the slave ring you broke up, the Reverents—"

"Old stories," said Lilith firmly. "Exaggerated old stories."

"Look," said Gavin. He reached behind his back and pulled out a crossbow like Lilith's, and held it out to her. "Mum told me about yours, so I made my own."

Lilith looked at it for a few seconds, and then took it.

"Hand-milled," she mused, peering along the barrel. "Fair job."

"I practise every day," he said. "I can hit the end of a twig from twenty metres."

Lilith gazed at him.

"A twig isn't the same as a person," she said quietly. She shook her head. "No. Stay away, keep your head down, look after your family. Let someone else worry about the world."

"But Thorsen—"

"Thorsen's just one in a line. There were Thorsens before. He's not even the worst."

She handed the crossbow back as Juliet walked in.

"Dinner in twenty minutes," said Juliet, smiling. Then she saw the crossbow and her face became still. She said brightly, "No weapons in the house. That's the rule, isn't it, Gavin?" She looked at Lilith. "And you too."

"Sorry," said Lilith. "My fault."

"Sorry, Mum," muttered Gavin.

Juliet nodded. "Remember when you shot yourself?" she asked.

Gavin ducked his head and looked embarrassed. "Mum, that was *years* ago," he moaned.

"Oh, yes. Practising his quick-draw. Triggered it by accident and shot a hole right through the jacket. Shot himself in the bum, isn't that right, darling?"

"*Mu-um.*"

Juliet smiled, but her eyes were angry. "You wave those things around, someone gets hurt. That's what they're for." She looked at Lilith as if about to say something else, but instead turned and walked out.

Gavin glowered at the floor. "Someone's got to do something," he muttered. Lilith didn't answer, and he stalked away, bristling with anger. Lilith closed her eyes.

Cora followed Juliet through to the kitchen and found her scrubbing a pan as if trying to grind right through it.

"Are you all right?" she asked. The woman jumped.

"Oh! Hello, my love. Yes, of course." She wiped her face with her sleeve. "Just thinking about that jacket. Ripped right through it, so he did, foolish boy. Good one too; leather. He was so cross, he wanted to throw it away."

She smiled at Cora. "He's a good boy, but he gets angry, he stops thinking. Reckons you can tear down the world and somehow it will sort itself out. Smash it all down and rebuild, eh? Daft. Can't rebuild with dust."

She shook her head. "He's still got the jacket, you know."

"He didn't throw it away?"

"No, it was a good coat, I told him so. Silly to waste it. I found a scrap of leather and replaced the panel, good as new." She looked down at the pan and sighed. "Foolish boy."

On the third day, Kai went into Base to catch up with friends, and Cora spent the afternoon on the roof. When she came down, Lilith was out of bed.

Lotty was chopping vegetables, and Juliet and Lilith sat at the kitchen table. Lilith gave Cora a stiff nod. Juliet watched Cora's face.

"My sister never knew when to take it easy," she said.

Lilith gave a thin smile. Everything about her seemed tight, as if she'd tied herself up with straps. "We have to keep moving," she said. "Eventually they'll realise we made it to Base. We need to be gone by then."

"She's like an iron bar," said Juliet. "Never bending, not a millimetre of give. Me, I was always more of a wavy tree." She laughed. "I always gave way in the end. I bet you're the same, right?"

Cora nodded.

"That's OK," said Juliet. "The tree bends, and straightens when the wind stops. Things that won't bend are stronger…" She glanced at her sister. "Till they snap."

Lilith looked down. After a second, she gave a small nod.

"That's enough exercise for one day." She stood up carefully. "Gavin said he knew someone who could help with cells."

Juliet's expression darkened. "My boy knows a lot of folks. Some of them ain't too good for him."

"I just need him to give me an introduction."

"He might give you a name, but he's not going anywhere with you, Lilith Castillo," said Juliet. Her face was suddenly very different, and her voice too: harsher, sharper, like a shard of bone. "Gavin's a fine brave boy, and he's looking for a cause. He'd follow you anywhere, if I let him. But I won't. You're welcome here as long as you like. I'm glad to have you. But when you leave –" Juliet

166

jerked a thumb at the door "– you won't take my family with you. *Understood?*"

Cora and Lotty watched, shocked. Suddenly it was easy to see Juliet as Lilith's sister, and the hard line of her lips didn't seem like those of someone who bent in the wind. The sisters glared at each other, but it was Lilith who backed down.

"Just a name then," she muttered.

Juliet sniffed. "I dare say he'll be able to help. Lotty, those onions are burning."

"Sorry, Mum."

Lilith left.

Glory Lights

Lilith grew stronger every day. She still slept a lot, but in the evenings she joined them for dinner, sitting carefully and eating small portions. Cora checked her stitches each morning.

"How does it feel?" she asked.

"It's fine."

Cora shook her head. "You're trying too hard. You're going to relapse, or tear the stitches again." But Lilith just shrugged.

"We have to leave," she said.

Kai started going out into Base more often. He wanted to bring Cora too, but Lilith forbade it. It was the first time Cora had really seen Kai cross. When he was at Juliet's he seemed distracted, and Cora thought he was probably going to leave for good soon, to his own friends and life. So while Lilith slept, Cora read. Lotty showed her a shelf full of schoolbooks and Cora devoured them one by one, science, history, geography – the world of Colony.

She hadn't realised how small Colony was, just a tiny dot on one continent. The Glories had landed here and found the humans, and no one quite knew how or why. The Glories looked like humans, but … *better*. Smarter, stronger, never sick, able to talk to each other over huge distances, fly… They lived lives of comfort and happiness, protected by the mysterious Lady Nostic. They were like gods.

And then one day they were gone, and even the memories of them, mostly. The humans awoke alone; hungry, cold, vulnerable, scraping through a century of devastation and loss before civilisation had restarted. And even that was down to the Glories – their machines kept the few survivors alive, gave them food and heat and light, and tiny clues on how to start again.

Who were the Glories? What were they like? Why had they come? Why did they *leave*?

Cora consumed the books, flicking through their pages at a speed that made Juliet laugh. But it was the world she was consuming, a world Lilith had told her nothing about. She read while Lilith slept, but not when she was awake; she realised that she didn't want Lilith to know. Lilith had hidden Colony from Cora. She'd hidden her family, her life, even her own *name*. She'd kept the world a secret.

Now Cora had her own secrets.

Cora sat in the garden. It was a nice day, with a pale-blue sky, and she could see the large Glory buildings in the centre, and Sanctuary, the Reverent headquarters, rising above them all, shining white. Kai hadn't returned last night, and she wondered if he was over there now – meeting friends, seeing Base, taking part in the world…

Lilith came out, carrying a chair. She was walking carefully, but Cora could tell she was feeling better and that the stitches were no longer bothering her. She looked like she was made of steel again. She sat next to Cora, and they watched the city.

After a while, Lilith pointed. "That's the power supply."

Cora looked and saw a Glory building with a domed roof like half a nutshell. Lilith said, "The Glories laid down the power and water grid. Power comes from a big shaft. They send water underground. It's very hot deep down, and the water comes back as steam and drives a machine."

Cora was bemused. Lilith caught her look and seemed embarrassed. "I'm just explaining why it's hard to get power cells here. No one needs them."

"OK…"

"It's not a big deal."

"OK."

Lilith nodded and gazed off in another direction. Cora cast about for something to say.

"You're looking better," she tried.

Lilith nodded. "I think that Glory medicine is still working inside me. Hurts on the inside, but they were good stitches. Neat job. You, ah… You did well."

Cora tried not to look surprised. "Thank you," she managed.

"No problem."

There was another pause. Then Lilith said, "I'm not always easy to get along with."

Cora's mouth fell open in surprise.

"I can be a little … *focused*," said Lilith. "And sometimes that can seem like I don't care about people. About … you."

"It's OK," said Cora. "Really, you don't have to—"

"It's just that I have to make sure you're safe. That's my job."

They sat in silence. *Your job*, thought Cora. *Is that what I am?*

"Hey!" came a voice, and Cora looked up to see Kai's beaming face.

171

"Hey," she said, smiling. She hadn't been sure he would return, and felt a sudden wave of relief at seeing him.

Lilith scowled. "Hmph," she muttered. "Not dead then."

"And it's lovely to see you too," said Kai, grinning. "Came to rescue Cora. It's Glory Lights tonight, remember?"

"What's that?" asked Cora.

"Big party. Lots of folk, free food, and they show off the decorations for Glory Day. It's brilliant. You'll love it."

Lilith frowned. "Cora shouldn't go out. We don't know who's watching."

Cora's heart sank.

"Oh, Lily," said Juliet, coming out from the house. "Let the child go. No one has come looking for you, and from what you've said they all think you're in Sheen."

"Yes, but they might see her."

"A crowd's the best place to hide. And the neighbours have seen her about – it would look strange if she didn't go."

"Well…"

"Besides," said Juliet. "You and I have some catching up to do. I've got a bottle of rum here that needs a friend, and Cora will just cramp our style."

Lilith rolled her eyes. "You always were a bad influence,"

she complained.

Juliet smiled. "Gavin and Lotty are going too," she said. "You four stick together, OK?"

"Oh," said Kai, slightly crestfallen. "I thought I'd show Cora the sights a bit."

"That's nice," said Juliet. "You'll do it all together." She gazed steadily at Kai until he dropped his head.

"OK," he said, sighing.

"So, what decorations?" asked Cora.

"Just you wait," said Kai, his face lit up again. "You're going to *love* it."

That evening Cora, Kai, Gavin and Lotty wrapped up in thick coats and stepped out into the snowy town. It was busy; people streamed from every house, heading towards the central square, waving and calling cheerful hellos as they passed. At first Cora flinched and hid between Kai and Gavin; but there were too many to avoid, and they all made their greetings and moved on. Gradually she relaxed, even began to enjoy herself. The cheerfulness was infectious.

They reached a large square with tall Glory buildings on each corner, and one street leading off towards the Sanctuary halls. The crowd was huge here, thousands strong, and Cora felt nervous again, but Kai guided her through the revellers to a point ten metres from a stage in front of the largest building.

"It's even busier than last year!" he shouted in delight. The crowd filled the square to its edges and swayed in all directions, laughing and bustling. On stage, men and women were smiling and waving to the crowd. The one in the centre was smartly dressed in a thick black fur coat, brown silk scarf and a fur hat, with polished brown boots. His face was round and cheerful and slightly shiny.

"GOOD EVENING, EVERYONE!" he shouted. His voice boomed around the square from all directions at once, and the crowd cheered back at him.

"That's Governor Thorsen," whispered Kai in her ear. Cora stared at the man as he beamed, and absorbed the noise from the crowd. He looked like he smiled all the time. As if smiling was his job. He held his arms open wide.

"WELCOME TO THE GLORY LIGHTS!"

The crowd clapped and cheered, and Governor Thorsen stepped up to a huge switch and flicked it on. The whole square lit up with bright-coloured lights, and the crowd roared.

There were lights on strings, lights in shapes. They were white and red and green and blue, steady and flashing, some fixed, some moving in patterns, fastened to wooden scenes that turned and swung. Cora watched with her mouth open in delight.

"Isn't it great?" asked Kai. "They do this every year. Look over there!"

Around the edge of the square was a series of stages, and the crowd shuffled between each one to look. The first one had a painted backdrop of the night sky. Lights moved down on a sliding wooden block, as if arriving from the sky, and there were models of people. They were tall, with silver clothes, and their faces shone with lights hidden inside them.

"That's the Glories arriving," said Kai.

The next stage was like a model of the whole Colony. It had Base, with the Sanctuary building and a few others, and Sheen, on its huge black wheels, and towards the back was the Recon tower. They were all lit up, and a little model train moved between them.

Then more stages, some of Base, some of Sanctuary, one of Recon surrounded by forests, some historical scenes that Kai explained, all perfect miniatures of lights and papier-mâché. And finally a stage that was taller than the others, so tall that Cora had to lean right back to see the top. At the bottom were more of the little figures, looking up just like she was. And behind them, the whole backdrop was a woman. Her cloak and long tumbling hair were like the night sky, black-blue and pricked with dots of light. Her face was kind, and one arm reached out over them.

Cora gazed at her. Kai said, "She's beautiful, isn't she?" He sounded serious. As Cora watched, he touched his hand to his forehead in a quick, almost automatic gesture.

"It's the Lady Nostic, isn't it?" said Cora.

Kai nodded. "They say the Lady Nostic looked after the Glories, before they left," he said quietly. "Some believe she's looking after us still."

The others in the crowd were all touching their heads, as he had done. Cora stared up at the stage.

"Yes," she said at last. "Yes, she's beautiful."

Kai nodded. Then he clapped his hands together. "Right! I'm hungry. Come on!"

Cora realised they'd gone right round the square and reached the Sanctuary building, and there was a fantastic smell of sausages and fried onions. The area in front of the building was full of tables heaving with food – warm bread rolls, salads, cooked meat and fish, steaming bowls of stew and vegetables.

"Let's find a place near the dancing!" Kai said. He grabbed Cora's hand and dragged her along between the tables and the crowd. She lost her grip on Gavin's arm and turned to protest, but Kai ploughed on, and eventually

176

found two seats next to a large wooden platform, where a heaving mass of people danced to a band playing fiddles and drums. Kai served Cora a plate of spicy sausages and cabbage, and they ate and watched.

"What do you think?" he bellowed.

"Brilliant!" The food was delicious and there seemed to be no end to it, more than Cora had ever seen in one place. People danced, sang, cheered, kissed, all around her. It should have been intimidating, but it wasn't. It was *exciting*! She tasted everything and sipped at a cup of hot mulled juice.

"Best meal of the year!" shouted Kai. He burped. "Gonna get more drinks. Back in a minute!" He stood and left Cora on her own, watching the fiddler grinning as he played his tunes. Lanterns flickered, onions fried, dancers whooped, and Cora was entranced, and so caught up in the moment that she didn't notice anyone, until...

Until a shadow blocked out the torchlight and a voice said, "Hello. Would you mind if I sat here?"

Conversations

Cora looked up to see an old man in a dark-brown robe, leaning against the table. He seemed out of breath.

"Would you mind?" he asked, gesturing to the seat beside her. "Just a moment, if I may. I think my dancing days are behind me." He smiled; his face was friendly, and his smile made Cora want to smile back.

"Um… Sure," she said. He nodded his thanks and sat on the bench next to her with a grimace.

"I could never resist dancing," he said. "Have you tried yet?"

Cora shook her head. "I don't know how."

His eyes creased. "I don't believe that's stopping anyone else, my child. Certainly not me." He reached for a clean cup and poured some beer from a jug on the table. His nose was crooked, as if it had been broken long ago. It gave him a cheerful appearance, and his thin neck and large, nearly bald head bobbed as he talked. Cora found herself nodding along with him.

"I'm Curator Perea," he said.

"Malenka," said Cora, remembering the name on her ID card. "Malenka du Pris."

"Glory be, Malenka!" He raised his cup to her, and she raised hers back.

"Glory be," she replied happily.

"And may the Lady Nostic uplift you."

"Oh! Er … and you."

He smiled and took a draught of the beer. "Oh, that's better." He gestured towards her plate. "Good food, yes?"

"Oh, *yes*," she said. "Best I've ever had!"

He seemed pleased. "We try. The church provides it. It's a good way to end the day. Reminds us of how much we've achieved – with the Glories' help, of course." He chuckled at the revellers. "And there's nothing like a free meal to bring the people out!" He buttered a roll. "Where are you from, Malenka?"

Cora bit her lip. "Um, out of town. I haven't been here before."

"Ah, an outsider! What do you think of our decorations?" He waved his butter knife at the stages and lights behind them.

"They're wonderful," said Cora, smiling. "I love the

Lady Nostic."

"Of course." He nodded seriously. "We mustn't forget her. We may have lost the Glories, but she's still looking out for us, yes?"

Cora frowned. "I suppose?"

The old man smiled. "Sorry. I can't help preaching – it goes with the robes, you know." His eyes twinkled. "You see, I love these celebrations, but they're only possible because of the Glories. Even now, their wonders give us the power to drive these lights, to prepare the food. A reminder of what they were to us. And a call to reclaim them – not just for one evening, but for all time. I think that would be worth anything, don't you?"

He leaned slightly towards her as he spoke, and Cora leaned back in response. He stopped and laughed.

"Oh, forgive me, please! I'm too much." He sat back. "I get too intense. Most of the year I'm cooped up in there." He pointed to the Sanctuary building behind him. "I don't meet many normal people!" Cora smiled back and relaxed. He watched the crowd.

"But then," he said, "you're not exactly normal, are you, Nadia?"

Cora frowned. "Malenka," she said.

He turned to face her, and shook his head. "Not Malenka," he murmured, gazing into her eyes. "And not

Cora either. And you *have* been here before, in Sanctuary. A long time ago."

Cora sat very still. She felt the hairs rise on the back of her neck.

"I should know," he said. "I held you in my own arms."

"There she is!" called a voice. Cora turned and saw Lotty and Gavin in the square, pointing. When she turned back the old man was walking away through the crowd.

"Stop!" she yelled, but he kept going. She chased after him but collided with Kai, who was holding two glasses full to the brim.

"Whoa – watch out!"

"Did you see him?" shouted Cora.

"Who?"

"The man in brown robes!"

Kai looked puzzled. "A priest? There's one over there," he said, nodding to one side. Cora looked, but it was someone else, a round, jolly man who was drinking from a beer tankard and laughing.

"Hey!" said Gavin. "What's up?"

The man was gone.

They walked back through the streets of Base in the dark. Others passed them, but Gavin didn't return their hellos. He glared at every corner as if waiting to be attacked.

Lotty wandered ahead of them, happily licking a toffee apple.

"And he said he was a curator?" asked Kai for the third time.

"Yes. I think he was telling the truth. He seemed … sincere."

"And you can't give us any better description? I mean, brown robes, bald – not much to go on."

"Shush, I'm concentrating."

And she was. She was trying to *look*; to follow the causes back from the moment he had sat down next to her. He hadn't been dancing, she realised; that had been a lie. In her mind she watched him walking purposefully towards her table. Before that he was standing at the edge of the crowd, watching. Then further back, and he was following them as they looked at the stages on the way to Sanctuary. And before that … he was waiting for them to arrive.

But she couldn't see anything beyond that, only a grey mist. Whatever caused him to wait, it was more than a day ago, further than she could see.

"Why would he be looking for you?" asked Gavin. "I thought it was the police you were hiding from."

Cora hesitated. "It's complicated," she said. "I don't really know." She shook her head. "We should tell Lilith."

Kai said, "If we do, she'll want to leave."

It was true. If Cora told Lilith that a *Reverent* had tracked her, found her, known her name —

her real name?

— she would make them run immediately. And then what would happen? Cora chewed her lip.

"Lilith's still recovering," she said at last. "She needs to heal. And this man… He already knew I was in Base; he was waiting for me. If he meant us harm he could have done it already."

"So, what?" asked Kai. "You want us to keep quiet?"

Cora sighed. "Yes."

Gavin studied her for a few seconds, and then nodded. "OK."

The lights were on in the kitchen when they reached home, and they found Lilith and Juliet sitting at the table, surrounded by the remains of a dinner and a half-empty bottle of rum.

They looked startled. Lilith seemed to have just been saying something, and when the children entered she turned to Juliet and they burst out laughing.

"Hello!" shouted Lilith.

"Hellooooo!" shouted Juliet.

Cora and the others exchanged glances. "Evening," said Kai cheerfully. "Been celebrating, have we?"

"Catching up," said Juliet. "It's been a while. Did you

have fun?"

"Yes," said Cora, "but I was tired, so they brought me home."

Gavin said nothing. Juliet smiled.

"Right you are, love. Easy day tomorrow. Goodnight, my darlings."

"G'night!" bellowed Lilith.

They said their goodnights and left the women. In the hall, Gavin turned to Cora. "We talk tomorrow," he murmured. His voice was low, but his eyes bored into hers. "Why they're looking for you, what's going on, the whole story, understand?" Cora nodded.

"Yes."

"Yes. Goodnight then."

Cora lay in the dark, thinking about the strange man and what had led him to her.

You have been here before, he'd said. *In Sanctuary. I held you in my own arms.*

Was he telling the truth? What did he know about her? *You're not exactly normal, are you?*

And a name: *Nadia.*

She fell into a restless sleep but awoke after an hour, thirsty. She went to the kitchen for a glass of water and saw that the light was on; Lilith and Juliet were still up.

She was about to enter when she heard her name. She paused just before the doorway.

"—a nice girl," said Juliet's voice.

"She is." Lilith, sounding tired.

"Helps around the house. Very polite. Not like you at all, really."

Lilith snorted. "Thanks, sis." A long pause. "Yours are good too."

"Gavin's a good boy." Juliet sniffed. "Gets angry sometimes. Always wanting to smash the system. Takes after his aunt, no doubt."

Another pause and a clink of glass. "Smart though," came Juliet's voice again. "When he does his schooling, he's smarter than I've ever been and he's not even half done yet. Fixed our hot-water system last winter."

Cora felt guilty, eavesdropping. But she didn't stop. It was fascinating, listening to Lilith talking about anything other than survival, or danger, or the need to hide. It was like a different woman.

"Got to say, Lil, I never had you as the mothering type."

"I guess not." Lilith's voice was muted.

"Too busy adventuring. You and Anish."

A sigh. "Yes. In those days. Not now."

"Seems to me…" There was a pause, and the *glug-glug* of a drink being filled. "The last time I saw you, you talked about a baby you were looking after."

Cora's ears pricked up. Juliet continued. "A *special* baby."

Silence.

"Lilith, what happened? Why did you go, why did you never come back? Is it because of her?"

Silence.

"You could stay in Base, you know." Juliet again. "It's bigger now, you could hide, get some ID, lie low."

Now Lilith spoke. "No. Sisal's hunting us. You know what she's like, she'll never stop. And what they could do, if they got her… She *is* special, Jules. She can do astonishing things. She can change the world. I mean, literally *change the world*. And she can't stop." Lilith's voice took on an urgent tone. "I try to tell her, but she just keeps *doing* things—"

Juliet laughed. "You tell a teenager to stop doing something, and you're amazed when she doesn't?"

"She doesn't *listen*!" protested Lilith.

"Remember what you were like as a girl?"

"That was different."

"Uh-huh."

"It *was*. I have to get her away from people. If she ever thought about how she could use this… She's too dangerous. And we *fight*! She wasn't like this before, we're

186

always *arguing*…"

"She's growing up, Lil!"

Another pause.

"Look." Juliet's voice, softer. "I don't really know what's going on. But you can't just make her do what you say. That's what happens with kids. First they worship you, then they think you're as stupid as mud. And then after a bit they come back, if you're lucky, and that's all you can hope for."

Then Lilith again, sounding wretched.

"I'm a terrible mother."

Cora blinked in astonishment. She'd never heard Lilith admit to being bad at anything. And – *mother*? "I can't do it. I see you with them. She already likes you more than me."

"Rubbish," snorted Juliet. "She never takes her eyes off you."

"I don't know what I'm doing."

"Why *did* you do it? Why did you take her?"

Cora leaned towards the doorway, holding her breath. *Take her?* She was *taken*?

When Lilith spoke, she seemed lost. "I don't know," she muttered. "We knew what they'd done to her. Anish said it wasn't right. He adored her. He always wanted a family. We talked about it but it was never going to happen, not

187

with our work. But he saw her, and he loved her. And then – and then he … he was *dead*, he was *gone*, and they took her too and, and… Oh, Jules, I miss him so *much*…"

Her voice disintegrated and there was nothing but an ugly crying sound, and Juliet's voice, soothing and calm.

Cora stepped back, aghast. The person making that sound wasn't anyone she knew. It wasn't Seleen, it couldn't be. Seleen had never admitted weakness. Seleen was indestructible, unbendable, indomitable. This … *Lilith* was something else – someone who had *taken* Cora, hidden her on the mountain away from everyone. Why? *Why?*

She couldn't listen any longer. She'd forgotten her thirst. She crept back to her bed and lay awake for a long time, staring at the ceiling.

The next morning, when Gavin emerged from his room, Cora was waiting for him.

"You said you knew about a warehouse," she said. "With power cells."

"Hi," he said.

Cora shook her head. "The warehouse," she insisted. "Can you show me?"

Gavin shrugged. "Sure, but you won't be able to get in. There's security, *Glory* security. No one can get in, not

188

even Lilith."

"Not Lilith," said Cora. "Me. You and me. And I *can* get in."

Keep your head down, Lilith had said. *Let someone else worry.* Lilith wanted to hide Cora away forever … but Lilith had lied. Lilith was a person Cora didn't recognise. And Cora was tired of seeing the world from a distance; it was time she made her own decisions.

"I'll tell you about last night," she said. "Why I think people are hunting us. I'll show you, and then…" She squared her shoulders. "And then you can show me how to make a difference."

Power

"Sisal's looking for *me*," said Cora. "And I think maybe the Reverents are too."

Lilith and Juliet were still asleep, and Lotty was in the kitchen eating breakfast. Cora sat with Gavin and Kai in Cora's room.

"Why?" asked Gavin.

"I don't know for sure." Cora bit her lip. "But it's probably because … I'm not … normal."

Gavin studied her. "You look normal."

"Cora," warned Kai, sounding serious for once. "Cora, I don't think you should—"

"Shut up, Kai. Look, it sounds weird, but I can see … *time*, in a way. A little bit. Like – after Curator Perea left, I could see that he had been waiting for me. It wasn't a guess; I could *see* it."

Gavin blinked. "What?"

190

"If something happens," she said carefully, "I can see what caused it. *All* the things that caused it." She took a deep breath. "And not just see... I can change things. Very tiny things, almost smaller than you can imagine. But they have an effect. I can change things in the past, so they end up different now."

Gavin's forehead wrinkled. "Is this a joke? I don't get it."

"It's not easy," said Cora. "I mean, it's really *hard*. I have to hold all the consequences in my head, everything that would be different. But I can—"

"What are you *talking* about?" he interrupted. "You can't change *time*! Can you?" He looked at her and Kai as if they were mad. "No! I mean, even if you could... You *can't*. Look, if you changed time, you'd be part of the changed events – which would mean you wouldn't be changing the past, you wouldn't even know you *had* changed the past, which would mean ... what?"

Cora shrugged. "I can tell. And so can people who are affected, a little. I'll show you – Kai, give me one of your dice."

Kai looked unhappy. "Cora, this is a bad idea," he muttered.

"He won't believe me otherwise."

"You know Lilith would say no."

191

"Lilith is—" snapped Cora, and stopped. *Lilith is not Seleen*, she'd been about to say. *Lilith is a stranger I don't recognise. Lilith lied to me.*

"Lilith is injured," she said at last. "It's my decision. Give."

Kai hesitated, but handed one over.

"Pick a number," Cora said to Gavin.

He frowned. "Three."

Cora rolled the die on to the table. It was a four.

She *looked* before the die had even settled. The previous time, she'd tweaked the nerves in her wrist, or the bounce off the ground. But now the path of the die through the air seemed clear and simple to her; she nudged it as it tumbled and let it land.

Two.

Again.

Three.

She gathered the threads together and *fixed* them. Three gold dots looked up at them.

Gavin stared at the die. Eventually he said, "What just happened?"

"It landed on four," said Cora. "But I fixed it."

His face screwed up. "Could be chance," he muttered.

Cora nodded. "Give me another die," she said to Kai. "Gavin, pick two numbers."

"Double-six," he said automatically. Cora rolled the dice and set to work.

Three-four.

The chance of rolling two sixes was one in thirty-six. She watched the dice as they fell, nudging them, and again. And again, and again.

Five-two. Six-three. Two-four…

She felt different this time, she realised. It was like returning to a previously unsolvable maths problem and suddenly seeing the answer. She let the possibilities flow across her mind, faster than before.

And within the flow, she saw the woman.

Just as before, she was a soft ghost in Cora's vision; smooth dark skin and thick short black hair. A neat white buttoned outfit that made Cora think of the medic back at Base. And green eyes, clear and calm but with that slight worried frown, as she said something just out of Cora's hearing…

Six-six.

Cora *fixed* the change in place and sat back. She had replayed the roll twenty-eight times, with no panic. She was becoming more powerful.

Gavin gaped at the dice. "I *felt* it," he muttered. "I felt them *change*…" He shook his head. "Glories' blood, they'd love you at the dice pits."

"It had occurred to me," murmured Kai.

Gavin looked up. "So you can make them be whatever you want?"

Cora shook her head. "No. I can go back, make tiny changes, and see what would happen. I have to keep trying until I see one that works."

"And does it just work with dice?"

"No." Cora looked straight at him. "I stopped a bullet firing," she said. "I saved Lilith's life."

You almost killed a man.

Gavin sat back in his chair, gazed at Cora, and rubbed his chin.

"Sisal wants me because of this," said Cora. "I don't know the details —" *Lilith won't tell me the details* "— but I'm pretty sure."

"Someone like you could change the world," mused Gavin.

"You think it needs changing," she said. He nodded. "Warehouse first," she said. "Get Lilith's cells."

Gavin examined the dice for a long time. "Lotty!" he called suddenly. "Time for school!"

He nodded.

"This evening."

When night fell, Gavin and Cora slipped out of the house

194

and on to the street. They were quiet, but as they were closing the door, a hand caught it. It was Kai.

"Me too," he murmured.

"No—" started Gavin.

"Or maybe we should check with Lilith?" asked Kai innocently.

Gavin grimaced. "OK. Quickly."

Cora almost smiled. In truth, she was a little relieved to have Kai with them. They left, Kai smiling and Gavin glowering behind him.

Gavin led them through the dark streets of Base to a large, dusty building deep in shadow, and down a flight of stairs to a cellar. From there, they seemed to enter another building. The houses here appeared to be a network of interconnected rooms and basements, and occasional squares of open air just a metre or so wide, like mineshafts.

"It's secure at the front," said Gavin, "but these old buildings are full of cellars. Mate of mine found this."

He opened a door and they emerged on to a narrow lane, opposite a dark metal door.

"This is it," muttered Gavin. "Quiet now."

They crept forward. Gavin opened the door to reveal a thin slice of pale-yellow light. He slipped inside, and the others followed. They were in a corridor. Dust had settled at the edges of the floor but not in the middle; someone walked here often. The air smelled cold and stale. Cora realised she could feel her heart beating.

"We're in the next building, underground," Gavin muttered. "There's a secure area inside, completely sealed, by order of Sisal herself."

A few metres along, he stopped at another door. This one was made of Glory material, smooth and white and impervious. To the right of it was a panel, and a small red light. Gavin pointed to the panel.

"It's a scanner," he whispered. "You put your hand against it, and it only lets you in if it's the right palm-print. It measures your pulse or something too. No one can get past it."

He gazed at her.

Cora blinked. She looked at the door, and the panel, and suddenly realised what he was saying.

"*I* can't open it," she said, baffled. "I can't." She shook her head. "You don't understand, I can't just *make things happen*. I can only go from effect to cause. If something happens, I can see what caused it. But it has to happen first."

"OK," said Gavin. "So I put my hand on it, something will happen, right? And then you change it."

"Well…"

Gavin's eyes bored into Cora. "We need you."

Cora hesitated. She had no idea what to do. But... *We need you.* No one had ever said that to her before. *We need you.*

She nodded and took a breath. "OK. Yes."

Kai put a hand on her arm. "Cora, are you sure about this?" He looked scared. "Lilith will kill us if she finds out. She'll kill *me* for letting you!"

"You're not *letting* me," Cora snapped. "I'm not under your control, or hers, understand? I make my *own* decisions."

She shook him off, stepped forward and pressed her hand hard against the scanner.

The red light started blinking right away. Then the panel beeped, once, twice, then gave a loud squawk – and somewhere in the building a siren wailed.

"Here we go," gulped Kai. But Cora was already *looking...*

She tried to ignore the siren, concentrating on the blinking red light. What made it blink? Something very tiny... She focused harder and saw a faint spark, a silver river running along a thin wire that led to the light. The river started and stopped, and the light blinked on and off. She followed it...

The wire came from a strange scrap of green plastic

inside the panel. Within the plastic raged a storm of effects too complex to make out, but the silver river was simple. She could tweak the wire, she thought. Just *snip* it…

Cora nudged at it, imagined it pinched and broken, and the red light stopped blinking. There. She smiled and watched this new reality play out, ready to fix it into place.

The siren was still wailing.

"Better be quick," muttered Gavin. He sounded tense.

Swallowing, Cora *looked* again. The siren shrieked at her, horrible and shrill, and her heart thudded in response. She forced herself to stay calm, and realised: the blinking light wasn't the problem, of course. It was the green plastic, with its thousands of signals. But no – it was getting a signal from somewhere far away, from an even *more* complex machine. *That's* what was making the alarms ring.

"Cora, *come on*," moaned Kai.

Cora raced along the timeline of the signal, trying to understand, but it was too hard, too hard! It was like trying to lift a heavy boulder, too heavy, and nowhere to get a hand-hold – a sick, nervous feeling of failure. And in the *now* time, she could feel the consequences spiralling out of control, more alarms starting, a sound of running feet…

She *looked* at the signal from the green plastic to the larger machine. It wasn't like the blinking light wire, she realised. This one was a pattern of tiny light pulses, incredibly complex – *that* was the problem. The pattern was wrong. But the pattern was made of thousands of points, *millions* – how could she possibly make it right?

"Hurry up!" hissed Gavin. "The guards are coming!"

She couldn't, Cora realised with sick dread. She couldn't make it right.

She *couldn't.*

Secrets

The siren wailed.

"We have to go!" shouted Kai.

Cora peered desperately at the tiny green machine and the signal it was sending to the centre. In panic, she tried jamming or changing the pattern randomly, but it had no effect. *Concentrate.* A ghostly, familiar image appeared in front of her, and she shook her head to dispel it, screwed her eyes shut and opened them to see the scuffed floor by the doorway. Dust at the edges, she realised – no dust at the door itself. No dust...

Someone had gone through here recently, scuffing the dirt as they entered. She followed the scuff marks back in time to their cause – a guard, this morning. The dust had been disturbed by the guard going through. The guard could go through because the door had opened. The door had opened because *his signal was correct.*

Cora examined the signal. It was long, but she could see it clearly, spread over a sliver of time. She raced forward in time, to the moment she'd placed her own hand on the panel, saw her own signal … and *changed* it to the one before.

The central machine did something different. It sent back a new response, and said nothing to the sirens or other machines. Alarms stayed silent, the light flickered green, guards were not woken up…

Fix it fix it now fix it…

She *fixed* it into place, and reality changed.

"Whoa," muttered Gavin.

"Cora? Cora, are you all right?"

Cora looked up at Kai's worried face and grimaced. "Give me a minute," she hissed. A blot of red pain pulsed in her head.

"Come on," said Gavin. "Before it locks again."

He slipped through the doorway. Kai helped Cora stagger behind them.

There was another doorway on the left, and a set of metal steps leading down to the right. They took the steps. Again, the floor was dusty, with a path kicked through. Something about the dust bothered Cora, but she couldn't think what.

They reached a storage area filled with steel containers.

Each container was locked. Gavin pulled a small bundle of metal hooks from his bag. He selected two, inserted them into the keyhole, and, with a look of great concentration, started moving them around.

The others waited. Gavin was struggling. He cursed as he dropped one hook and had to start again. After another minute, Kai rolled his eyes and nudged him aside. Gavin looked surprised but gave Kai the hooks, and Kai carefully moved one, then the other, then twitched both hands suddenly. The lock sprang open.

"Cora's not the only one with tricks," he murmured, smiling. They opened the door.

The container was full of power cells.

They were stacked in columns, and each one showed its tiny green indicator light, fully charged.

"Wow," breathed Kai.

"There must be a thousand cells here," whispered Gavin. "I thought there'd be, like, a hundred or something. Are they *all* like this?"

Cora looked across at the other containers. Fifty containers, at least. Fifty thousand cells, all fully charged… She shook her head. "I don't understand. I thought there was a shortage?"

Kai was gazing at the cells, and now he gave a strange smile.

"Power," he said. "That's what this is."

Cora frowned. "Well, yes. That's the point?"

Kai shook his head. "No, out there." He waved one arm. "Out there, there's a power shortage. Base and Sheen use grid power. The government controls it and no one can do anything without it. But if you had enough cells, you could be independent. Out of their control."

"But there's a shortage of power cells," said Cora.

Kai waved an arm at the containers. "Does this look like a shortage? Have a dozen. Have a *hundred*. They don't even have tracking devices attached. The power shortage is a *trick*." He grinned and slapped the top of the container, raising a small cloud of dust. "It's genius!"

Cora didn't understand why Kai was so delighted, but she shrugged, watching the dust drift on to the ground. There was something about that, wasn't there? About dust. The dust at the doorway, disturbed by the guard. By the guard entering that morning…

"Oh no," she gasped. "The guard!"

Kai stopped smiling. "What?"

"I saw a guard coming in, this morning. I mean, in my mind I *saw* him. That's how I got the door to work – I copied his signal." Oh, you *fool*. "The dust was disturbed by him walking in."

Gavin frowned. "So?"

203

"Walking *in*," said Cora. "Not *out*. Which means—"

"He's still here," muttered Kai.

Gavin brought out his crossbow.

"No one panic," he said. His voice stayed calm and firm. He looked up at the gantry and turned in a circle, pointing the crossbow. "We just have to get out, nice and slow. I'll lead, then Cora, then Kai. Ready?"

They nodded. Gavin grabbed some cells and stuffed them into his bag, and then crept towards the stairs. Cora followed them and tried to prepare herself to *fix* if she had to. They climbed back up to the gangway and towards the entrance, stepping carefully against the metal floor. Nearly there…

A man walked out of the doorway further on and stopped, staring at them in surprise. He was young, with a straggly ginger beard. He was holding a sandwich in one hand.

"What the—"

Gavin fired his crossbow and the bolt smashed into the guard's shoulder, spinning him around. He collapsed and roared in pain. Gavin stepped forward, reloading the crossbow, but the man grabbed it suddenly. Gavin gave a shout of alarm and it fired again, straight at the man's head—

"No!" shouted Cora.

Automatically, she reached *back* to the trigger point. It was hard, but easier than with the gun before. And she knew what she was trying to do this time. The trigger released the high-tension cable, forcing the bolt forward, and she *changed* it…

The cable *twanged* as it slipped off the bolt. Gavin and the guard gaped at it in astonishment, then the guard passed out, clunking his head against the metal floor. Cora, Kai and Gavin stared at the guard, and then at each other.

"Now what?" asked Kai.

"Come in, Five," came a voice.

Cora almost screamed. The voice sounded disjointed and faint. "Five, hello, respond, please."

She realised the words were coming from a radio on the guard's belt.

"Five is silent, repeat: Five is silent. Alert red."

A siren wailed above their heads.

"*Go!*" shouted Kai.

They ran. Sirens were going off in the corridor too, and red lights flashed on the walls. They raced back towards the exit. Cora's blood pounded. The guards would find them in no time, perhaps they already had, perhaps they were behind them now, she couldn't look back, run-run-run—

They burst out into the lane behind the warehouse and sprinted away. A voice behind them shouted, "Stop!" Two men were running out of the next warehouse along.

"Halt!" they roared. One raised a gun. "Halt or we fire!"

"This way!" called Gavin, and peeled off on to a side street. Cora and Kai raced to keep up with him. A brick next to Kai exploded into dust and he yelped.

"Head to the market!" shouted Gavin. But at the next junction Kai grabbed Cora's hand and pulled her in a different direction.

"Down here!" he hissed. He leapt down steps and around a corner, away from Gavin, with Cora in tow. Boots clattered behind them. Kai swung into what seemed like a dead end but there was a rubbish bin against one wall, and he used it to clamber up and over. Cora scrambled after him and down into a poky, narrow lane.

"Where are we going?" she called. Kai half turned.

"A safe place!"

The boots seemed further away. Kai pulled her into a recess between two walls and towards a tiny door, almost invisible. It led into a narrow corridor with round windows.

Kai slowed to a walk. "This way," he whispered. The corridor seemed to be made of Glory material, but worn.

The walls were slightly greasy, as if thousands of people had brushed past them, and the floor was scuffed. Kai led Cora to another door, taller and more ornate, with a carving in the shape of a star. Putting a finger to his lips, Kai leaned his ear against the door. After a moment he nodded and looked at Cora. His face had a strange, earnest expression.

"This is a safe place," he said.

She nodded. "OK."

"I just wanted to…" He shook his head. "Never mind. Come on."

He opened the door and ushered Cora inside.

It was an old, cluttered room, lined with polished wooden panels and hung with paintings. A window at the back illuminated a large desk piled high with books and paper. Wood burned in a fireplace against one wall.

A man sat at the desk, writing; when they entered, he looked up. He had a thin neck and wisps of grey hair, and he wore a brown robe. His nose was crooked, as if it had been broken a long time ago. He blinked at them in surprise from behind a pair of thick spectacles.

"Nadia!" he said. "Nadia, you came back!"

It was the priest from the festival.

Cora stood still.

"I'm sorry," said Kai from behind her.

Curator Perea

Cora's first instinct was to run. Push Kai aside, escape back out into the crowd, try to find the marketplace and Gavin, risk capture by the guards. But she held herself still, as Lilith had taught her; held still until she knew what she was facing.

What she was facing seemed to be an old man with a crooked nose and a kind smile, leaning back in his chair. Curator Perea, she remembered. He was beaming at her with an expression of gentle delight.

"My dear," he said, removing his glasses. "Welcome, welcome!"

He stood and walked around his desk, stopping well away from her as if she were a frightened animal. "Please excuse the mess – I had no idea we would meet again so soon!"

Still Cora didn't move. Kai was behind her, between

her and the door.

"How long?" she asked. "How long has Kai been helping you?"

Perea didn't answer. Cora nodded. "The whole time, of course. Stupid of me."

Kai said, "Cora, I was trying to help—"

"*Shut up,*" she snapped, without looking at him. He fell silent.

"I apologise for the subterfuge," said Perea. "You must forgive Kai—"

"The flyer," said Cora. "That was you; you gave it to him. And he found us, in Recon, and arranged the escape from Sheen. And he didn't leave when we reached Base. And he brought me to you at the Glory Lights." She shook her head. "And the dice game? Was that a set-up too? And the fall from the tree?"

"I really did fall," said Kai. "You saved my life. But... I *was* looking for you."

"And you pretended to be my friend."

"I *am* your friend—"

"You were my *handler*!" She whirled to face him. "I was your *job*! You're just another person treating me like *cargo*!"

Kai stepped back.

Perea coughed. "Please, Nadia, forgive us—"

"*My name is not Nadia!*"

He stopped.

"I'm leaving," she said. She glared at Kai until he moved aside, and walked to the door. "You can't stop me."

"Please!" Perea raised his hands. "I'm an old man; I couldn't stop you even without your powers. But please – I've waited thirteen *years* to find you again. And you are so like your mother."

Cora stopped with her hand on the door handle and closed her eyes. She should leave. She should *leave*.

"Yes, I sent Kai," Perea said. "To find you, to protect you, to make sure you reached Base. He gave up his home to search for you, so that you could understand who you are. *What* you are. *Please*."

Cora cursed, released the handle and turned back. She ignored Kai.

"Tell me then," she growled.

"Thank you." Perea sighed and leaned against his desk. "What do you know of your parents?"

"They're dead. They asked Lilith to look after me."

He looked thoughtful. "Hmm."

"And Lilith doesn't trust Reverents," said Cora.

"Lilith doesn't trust many people," he responded, smiling.

"Maybe she's right."

Perea didn't argue. Instead, he said, "May I…" He stopped, and smiled as if embarrassed. "I'm sorry. It's ridiculous – I'm trembling, look! It is *extraordinary* to see you again. And the things Kai has told me about your powers… Please, may I see?"

Cora snorted. "You brought me here to do magic tricks?"

He raised a hand. "I know, I have no right to ask. But I've searched for so long. Please?"

Cora drummed her fingers against her leg. Perea gazed at her as if he could hardly believe she was there. The hope on his face was compelling, somehow.

She glared at Kai. "Give me some credits." He looked surprised but reached into his pocket and handed her five coins. She tossed them into the air and let them fall to the ground.

"Heads," she said. As soon as the first coin landed, she *looked*.

It felt easier every time. The coins tumbled through the air, and she nudged them into shape and looped forward to see the results, over and over again, with hardly a thought. They landed in front of her and she *fixed* them.

She didn't look at them. She watched Perea, as he stared.

211

"Glory be," he whispered. "What are the odds of that?"

"For five coins?" Cora shrugged. "One in thirty-two."

"And for more? Twenty, say?"

"One in one million, forty-eight thousand, five hundred and seventy-six," said Cora.

Perea raised an eyebrow.

"Tell me," he said, "how many panels are there in the corridor outside?"

Cora was puzzled – what did that have to do with anything? But she answered: "Seventeen."

"And how far is it from this room to your cabin?"

"One thousand, five hundred and thirteen point six three kilometres."

"And the colour of the hair of the woman in your dreams?"

"Black," said Cora, and then blinked. "I mean—" She stopped and stared at Perea. "How did you know about her?" she whispered.

Perea laughed. "Cora, do you realise how extraordinary you are?"

Cora frowned. "Lilith says I'm good at maths."

"I suspect you are good at everything! The woman you see – does she say anything? Do you know who she is?"

"No," said Cora cautiously. "She speaks, but I can't hear her. I thought she might be..." She stopped. "My mother, maybe."

But Perea shook his head. "I'm sorry. Lilith told you the truth, about this at least. Your parents died many years ago."

Cora looked down. She'd known, in her heart, but still…

"They were Reverents, did you know that?"

"No," she said, shocked.

Perea nodded. "Oh, yes. Seekers – searchers for lost Glory technology. And they found something…" He clapped his hands suddenly. "Come! Let me show you. Kai, could you…?"

Kai nodded and left ahead of them.

"This way, my dear," said Perea. He limped out into the corridor with her. Kai walked a few metres in front, and occasionally held out a warning hand as someone passed ahead of them.

"We must be discreet," murmured Perea. "The Reverents were once a force of social justice – the Government's conscience. But some of my colleagues have wandered from their path. They think too much of finances, and a seat at the Governor's dining table. They like the stories of miracles, but would be terrified to witness one, and if they saw you…" He shook his head. "I fear they would hand you over."

213

They reached a heavy iron door, and Perea unlocked it and ushered Cora in. Kai stayed outside. Inside was a small room, dimly lit, decorated with carved wooden friezes with scenes from Colony's history, and filled with cases and stands.

"These are some of the most sacred pieces the church possesses," Perea whispered.

Some pieces were whole, while others seemed to be parts of larger devices. Some had markings and letterings. "Module 36-C", said one. "900W", said another. One, a small, coin-shaped device, glowed a soft green.

"Does it glow all the time?" asked Cora.

"No," said Perea. "I've only ever seen it light up once before." He moved on.

There were books, crudely cut and bound with thick grey thread that Cora thought might be catgut. The writing was dense and faded. "Written after the Fall," said Perea. "We don't know how long after. There was chaos for so long."

He led Cora to a tiny cell that contained a single display.

"You know of the Lady Nostic," he said. "Officially, she has no form. She's often portrayed as the night sky. But there is one single image of her. It is our greatest secret."

He pressed a button, and the display lit up.

"Oh," breathed Cora.

It was the woman from her dreams.

Black-haired, smooth-skinned, white-robed; perfect. She stood in a white room and her mouth moved as if she were speaking, though no sound came out. She was beautiful. Cora turned to Perea in wonder, and he smiled and pressed another button.

"—do not update your avatar," said the woman. Her tone was calm but forceful, a voice describing important instructions without panic. She had a strange accent, warm but precise. Her teeth were perfect.

"Disconnect if safe to do so, and assemble," she said. "This is a system-wide emergency broadcast to all users—" The picture flickered and then returned to the start. "—do not update your avatar. Disconnect if safe to do so…"

Perea pressed the button again and the display went dark. He touched a hand to his head and bowed softly, and Cora felt a strange urge to do the same.

"This was found shortly after the Fall," he murmured. "She describes an emergency. She says to disconnect, but we don't know what from. Who are the Users? What is an Avatar?" He shrugged. "The books say that the first of the Fallen could still see her, in their dreams, but their children could not. But you do, don't you?"

Cora gazed at the display. "Yes," she whispered.

Perea nodded. "Come. There is one more thing to show you."

He led her back into the main chamber, to something that looked like a narrow bed, sitting on a cream base and cushioned in a smooth, pale-green material. There was a panel on each side, and a thin metal arm that looked as if it could swing over the bed.

"Most of these were destroyed in the Fall," he said. "None of them work. One was even stolen from here –" he glanced at her "– thirteen years ago."

"What is it?"

"My colleagues believe it is a healing device. But your parents understood its true purpose."

A soft rap at the door stopped him. "We must go," he murmured.

Kai was waiting for them outside. Footsteps echoed from further inside the building, and Perea nodded; they headed back. Kai glanced at Cora as they walked, but she ignored him.

Back in Perea's room, he limped to his seat and leaned back.

"Tell me, Cora," he said. "Who were the Glories?"

Cora frowned. "I don't know."

"No." Perea shrugged. "We know they came to this world, and found the humans here. We know they took our shape, to look like us. We know they looked after us … and without them, we are bereft.

"But who were they? Where did they come from, and why? And why did they leave?" He sighed. "These questions vexed me, Cora, but I had no answers. Until one day, some years ago, two young Seekers came to my door.

"The Seekers had found a machine; a bed, like the one I showed you. But not like the others, lifeless and broken. This bed was still functioning. It was *alive*. They asked for my help to understand it, and gradually we realised that it held an extraordinary secret. It told us who the Glories really were."

Perea leaned forward and his eyes gleamed.

"Cora, *they were us.*"

Cora stared at him in confusion. "What?"

"Us," he repeated. "*Humans. We* were the ones who came to this world, who settled, who built Colony. *We* were the Glories! Us!"

Cora shook her head. "No, the Glories were … were *gods*. We can't do what they did."

"Not now," he agreed. "But once we could! Before the Fall, when we were still extraordinary!"

He smiled. "We thought the beds were for healing, but they're much more than that. They can *change* a person

217

– change them inside, to give them incredible abilities. To perform fantastic calculations, remember things with perfect recollection, talk to machines… The Glories were us, but *better*. Wiser, smarter, able to travel between the stars. They used these machines to *Uplift* themselves. To fill themselves … with Glory."

His voice trembled slightly.

"But something went wrong. We don't know what, but some disaster caused the machines to fail, and us too. The machines had minds, of a sort – the Seekers called them *processors* – and they were connected to each other. When the Fall came, they all failed together. We lost everything. We forgot the truth.

"But in this one device, the processor was disconnected at the exact moment of the Fall. And so it survived."

Perea's mouth twisted into a crooked smile. "It has only a single charge – a single program, it was called, the one it was using when it disconnected. The Seekers realised it would work only once – they could Uplift only *one* person. And it had to be a child, someone whose mind was still developing.

"They had a baby girl. Her name was Nadia."

Perea gazed at her.

"My parents?" breathed Cora. "It was them? *They* did this?"

He nodded. "This was their gift, you see? They made you a *Glory*. They gave you the powers the Glories possessed – and something more: an extra power, named *Consequences* – the ability to see from effect to cause, back in time."

Cora shook her head. Her parents had stood next to that bed, she thought. They had laid her down, and she had looked up at them, as they turned her into something else.

"What happened?" she asked.

Perea sighed. "At first we didn't know if it had succeeded. The results were hard to decipher. I worked with my assistant, a man named Reeve, for weeks before we were sure." His face darkened. "But Reeve was a traitor. He told Protector Sisal, and they attacked; your parents were killed, the machine stolen … and you were taken.

"I have spent thirteen years searching for you, Cora, knowing that my carelessness and naivety led to your parents' death, and your loss."

Shadows seemed to reach from the corners of the room as he spoke, and Cora imagined the old man's life since, shuttered away with his regrets. He shook his head.

"But now you have returned. And the possibilities, Cora! You see, we were *wrong*, your parents and I. It was only when I fully deciphered the results that I understood. We made you a Glory, but only a *fraction* of one – the process was unfinished. Now we can complete your transformation!"

"But you said the machine was stolen," said Cora.

"The machine, yes," he said eagerly, "but not the *processor*. I kept that separate, and even Reeve didn't know about it. The machine is only the vessel – the processor is everything, and I still possess it. Your abilities are only the tiniest scrap of your potential. Imagine it magnified a thousandfold. Imagine if you could see back, not just a day, but a week, a month, a year, a century – more! We can complete the Uplift and make you a *true* Glory!"

He raised his hands. "And I would *beg* it of you."

The tiniest scrap, thought Cora. The things she'd done, could do. *The tiniest scrap*. What would Lilith say?

She shook her head. "I'm not sure…"

"Think, girl!" exclaimed Perea. "Think what you could do for *all* of us, if you had these powers!"

"How? I can't fix the machines. I can't make other people Glories. I can't—"

"Don't you see? I've spent my life studying the Glories, trying to restore fragments of their world after the Fall. But you…" Perea's face was flushed. "*You could prevent it from ever happening!*"

220

Mortals

Curator Perea beamed.

"Imagine!" he said. "You could change the world. You could prevent the Fall from ever happening!"

"What?" Cora stepped back in alarm. "How? I can't do that!"

"Don't you understand?" he asked. "The Glories never left. *We* were the Glories all along – human beings, with machines. And then something went wrong – some disaster that broke the machines, and the humans too. But you, with your powers – you can go back and stop it. You can save them!"

"You don't understand," said Cora. "I can't do anything like that. I can only see a few hours back – a day at most. And I can only change tiny things; nothing like that!"

Perea smiled. "That's because you are not fully *Uplifted*

221

yet. We can complete the process and give you that power."

"But…" Cora shook her head. "But even if I could do that, this world will be *gone*. If I stop the Fall, everything will be different. Everyone alive right now will be gone, we won't *exist*. I can't do that!"

Perea nodded. "Yes. It seems unthinkable. And yet…" He sighed and looked about his office. "I am old, child. I've spent my life here in Sanctuary. I've been an acolyte, delivering food to the needy. I've been a scholar, I became a Seeker, and then a Curator. I have watched Colony grow. I have devoted my *life* to it. I love these people. But do you think they *want* these lives, surviving on scraps of what we were?" He shook his head. "Do you really think they're happy?"

"But I can't take it away from them!" protested Cora. "And *some* are happy!"

"Kai's mother died when he was a child, because we lack Glory medicines," said Perea. Kai bowed his head. "The government uses Glory technology to oppress the people they are supposed to serve. This is a twisted, broken version of the world, Cora, and it breaks us too. I remember Gavin as a boy; he used to come to services. Now he would destroy the system, tear it down – and you would help him."

222

"Well … yes, to rebuild it—"

"Let's not rebuild it. Let's *return* it!"

Cora almost reeled at the idea. It was like Sheen; too big to hold in her head. *Prevent the Fall.*

"The machine can't make me powerful enough," she said, stalling. "There's no way it can work."

"Let us *try*," begged Perea. "Even if it fails, you could be *our* Glory. You would have such power – to undo wrongs, mend us, show us the right ways. You could save us all! *Please*, Cora."

Cora shook her head. "I need to think. It's too much. I'm sorry."

Perea opened and closed his mouth. For a moment she thought he was going to shout; he trembled and his jaw clenched. But he restrained himself with a visible effort. Eventually he shook his head.

"I understand," he muttered. "I dared to hope, but you were lost too long."

"I'm sorry," she said again. "I'll think about it." *The tiniest scrap.* Could she really? "I'm not promising. But I'll think."

A glimmer of hope flickered in the old man's face, and he nodded.

"Very well," he said. He coughed. "Quite right. Yes, think on it – the difference you could make, the power to restore *everything*, to bring back our Glory days, in your hands. *Please*."

Cora nodded. His hope was overwhelming, and she felt embarrassed. "I promise," she said. "I—"

Suddenly the door to Perea's office smashed open and crashed against the wall.

Splinters flew in all directions from the force of an explosion that blew the lock and handle across the room. Kai yelped as a sliver of wood stabbed his cheek, and Cora and Perea spun around. Lilith stood in the doorway, holding her crossbow pointed at Perea's head.

"If you move *at all*," she hissed, "I will kill you."

They stared at her in astonishment. A trickle of blood dripped from Kai's cheek.

"Cora, are you all right?" Lilith demanded.

"I'm OK!" said Cora. "Everything's fine!" She held up her hands and moved in front of the old man. "Look, it's OK."

"Hello, Lilith," said Perea.

Lilith ignored him. "Move away," she ordered Cora. "Where's Gavin?"

Cora realised with a flush of shame that she hadn't thought about him. "Isn't he back at the house?"

"I left to look for you," said Lilith.

"We got separated. Kai … brought me here."

Lilith swung the crossbow round towards Kai.

"I should have killed you in Recon," she snarled. Kai shook and put his hands up.

Perea stepped around from behind Cora. "Please, Lilith, calm down. There is nothing to fear here—"

"How *dare* you!" she shouted. "How dare you take her like this!"

"She has the right to know her past."

"That's not your decision to make! I'm her guardian!"

"No, Lilith," said Perea gently. "*I'm* her guardian. You were just her *bodyguard*."

"What?" asked Cora.

"Shut up," said Lilith. "They asked me to look after her!"

Perea said to Cora, "We suspected we were being watched, you see. We hired two bodyguards, the best around: Lilith and her partner, Anish."

"Shut up!"

"They were attacked," continued Perea. "Anish was killed, and your parents. And you were gone. Eventually, I realised that Lilith had taken you."

"Stop talking or I *will* kill you!" Lilith grabbed Cora's arm and dragged her back towards the shattered doorway. "We're leaving now. Don't follow, don't ever contact her, just leave us alone!"

Cora tried to pull free. "You can't say that!" she shouted. "It's my life!"

But Lilith hauled her into the corridor and away.

"She has the right to decide!" called Perea as they left. "She could save us all!"

Lilith bustled Cora on to the street outside. "What were you doing there?" she demanded. "Where did you go with Gavin?"

"I was just – I was helping him, that's all!" said Cora. "I think he's safe, they were chasing us—" Lilith pushed her down a side alley and round a corner. Cora shook her head. "Where are we going? The house is back there!"

"Away," snapped Lilith. "We have to go now, before they find us."

"Wait, wait—" tried Cora, but Lilith was moving too fast. "How did you find me, if you haven't spoken to Gavin?"

"It doesn't matter."

"It does! Stop!" Cora suddenly heaved back and forced Lilith to stop. "Tell me, *how*?"

Lilith blew a fierce, exasperated sigh. "I can just *tell*, OK? When you use your … powers, I can tell. I can *feel* it."

Cora blinked. "Really?"

"*Yes*. You were doing something in a warehouse.

226

Changing a machine, I could feel it. And a guard. Then coins, in that room, landing heads up. I can feel the changes when you make them, OK?"

She pulled Cora forward, and Cora was too shocked to stop her.

"Every time?" she asked, stunned.

"Yes, every time! Come on!"

"At the cabin," Cora muttered, thinking. "You walked all night through the snow. It was because you felt me change the dice."

"Move!"

Cora let Lilith push her along the street. "But why shouldn't I?" she asked. "I could make things better!"

"This? This is better?"

"Well, no, but—" Lilith turned her down another narrow lane. "But if I had more power I could look further back, really *fix* things. Perea says I could fix the *world*—"

"And what would you do with that power, eh? What would you do?" Lilith was panting and her face was red. She seemed to be holding back some furious eruption.

I could undo everything, thought Cora. Somehow that didn't seem the right answer. But what could she say to convince Lilith? What did Lilith want?

"I could—" She stopped. "I could save Anish."

The street was quiet; no one around at all. Lilith turned to Cora, her face blank with shock.

"What?"

"I know about him," mumbled Cora. "I heard you talking to Juliet. I know he died, and you, you…" *Loved him*, she wanted to say. *Cry over him still*. "Miss him," she ended lamely. She took a breath. "But I could save him. I could bring him back!"

Lilith stared at her. Her mouth moved a little. "You," she said at last. "You would do that?"

Cora nodded. "Yes. Yes, of course!"

"Bring him back, so he'd never been gone."

"Yes!"

"You would do that … *awful* thing to me?"

Cora frowned. "What?"

"You would…" Lilith shook her head. "You would take my life, and the things that happened to me, and the decisions I made and continue to make and the *consequences* of those decisions, and *rearrange* me into something you think is better?"

"No, you don't understand—"

"You would *toy* with us, bend us to your idea of happiness like *dolls*?"

Cora shook her head, baffled. "No, that's not what I meant—"

228

"What you do is *wrong*," snarled Lilith. "You take away people's rights to their own decisions!"

"Only bad ones!"

"With you deciding what's bad and good? You would be a god now? Would we *worship* you?"

"Why do you *do* this?" shouted Cora. She pulled free of Lilith. "Why do you make everything sound so *terrible* all the time?"

"Because I know power, child," hissed Lilith. "I know what it does, I *understand* it. You have this much −" she pinched her fingers together in Cora's face "− and you would have killed that guard back in Sheen. You didn't even *think* about him."

"He was going to kill you! He *did* kill you!"

"It doesn't matter!"

Cora flung her hands up. "It matters to *me*!"

"Then you're a fool."

Lilith stormed into the next street, and Cora, seething, raced around the corner after her and almost bumped into her. Lilith was standing still.

"What—"

"Something's wrong," muttered Lilith.

The street was empty and quiet. No one out late, no lights anywhere. And Cora realised the street behind them had been empty too. And the one before…

Lilith gripped Cora's shoulder. "Run."

"What?"

"*RUN!*"

She pushed Cora back the way they'd come, breaking into a run, and suddenly the whole street lit up. Two men in uniforms raced from a building towards them. Lilith fired her crossbow and the first one ducked; she leapt, landed on him and launched a kick into the other's face.

She grabbed Cora's wrist and dragged her away before the men could rise.

"Come on!"

"Get her!" shouted a voice.

They peeled off down a side street. Cora tried to run and *look* at the same time. Guards streamed after them; she shifted the muddy frozen ground from under their feet, just a little—

The first guard slipped and collapsed and dragged the second down with him. Others clambered over them.

"Stop it!" spat Lilith, running and rewinding her crossbow at the same time. "Concentrate!" They reached a crossroads. Guards were racing towards them from three sides, and Lilith hauled Cora up the only clear street. More guards waited at the next junction, armed and aiming but not firing. Cora felt a sudden sharp stab in her neck. She reached up and felt something sticking

230

out of it.

"Lilith?" she asked, and then her legs wobbled and she almost collapsed. Lilith turned and stared at her, then put her arm under Cora's shoulder and heaved forwards. Cora couldn't make her legs work properly, and thinking was hard, but there was something wrong with this chase, wasn't there? Why was no one firing?

"There's something wrong!" she tried to say, but her lips seemed fat and clumsy and disconnected. Lilith dragged her round another corner and into a dead end, a high wall blocking their way.

They were being herded, Cora realised. Guards pounded up behind them. Lilith half carried Cora towards the wall, bent down and hoisted her up and on to the top.

"Move!" she shouted. "Run! Get away!"

Cora tried to make her body do what she asked it. She rolled over the top of the wall and crashed down the other side. Lilith scrambled up behind her, then swore and slapped at her neck as a dart hit her. She jumped down after Cora but stumbled and fell.

"Move!" she managed. She got to her feet again, pulled Cora up, and pushed her away—

And stopped.

They were surrounded by guards. Lilith panted and

ducked her head, scanning from side to side. One hand crept towards the back of her belt.

"Best not," said a voice.

Two guards stood aside and a short, neat woman stepped between them. Her hair was blonde and cropped, her skin pale. Cora knew her immediately, though she'd only seen a glimpse on a hillside, long ago now it seemed. She recognised that piercing, freezing gaze at once.

It was Protector Sisal.

"I told them you'd make it over the wall," she said, nodding in approval. "No one believed me."

Cora's legs wobbled, and now she was sitting down with no recollection of moving. Her face felt numb. Lilith tried to run but the guards grabbed her and dragged her to the ground. The last thing Cora saw was Lilith, still fighting, under a pile of guards and flailing batons.

Then everything went dark.

Protector Sisal

"Cora? Cora, can you hear me?"

There was a thick musty blackness in Cora's mind, a cloud that blocked her thinking, but glimpses… Lilith's anger, the empty street, the chase, Lilith throwing her over the wall, Lilith fighting and the troopers' batons crashing down, again and again—

Lilith!

Cora opened her eyes and then screwed them up against a sharp white light. A shadow loomed over her.

"Good," said the shadow, and moved away. The white light returned.

Cora sat up and nearly tumbled over as a wave of dizziness swamped her. Her arms felt like lead and her hands were numb. She waited for the feeling to fade and then looked up.

She was in a white room, small and almost completely

featureless with smooth plastered walls. She was sitting on a low cot bed. To her right was a toilet and sink. The far wall was only two metres away and contained a single door, with no handle. There was a chair against the wall.

Protector Sisal sat in the chair.

"Hello, Cora," she said. "How are you feeling?"

Sitting down, Sisal's feet only just touched the floor. She wore a trim dark-grey jacket and skirt, and her face was small and neat. She sat perfectly still, back straight and hands folded on her lap.

"My name is Sisal," she said. "I am the Head of Protection, and my job is to keep you safe."

Cora coughed. Her throat felt clogged and sore. One arm had a sore point, covered with a small plaster. Her heart thumped with a chaotic beat. She shook her head and glanced at the door. Could she make it?

"Safe from what?" she croaked.

"Everything," the woman said. Her voice was precise, as if she pronounced each word in her head before speaking. "Not just you, of course. I protect all of Colony."

Cora's head ached.

"You will be feeling woozy," said Sisal. "You've been asleep for some time. It seemed a sensible precaution, given your … abilities."

Cora remembered the little dart at her neck, but

everything seemed grey and the room was moving slowly around her.

"Cora? Cora, can you hear me?"

Cora snapped awake again. Sisal smiled. "Cora, I need to show you something. There is a picture next to you. Look at it, please."

Cora moved her head in a long loop and saw the picture. It was like a drawing, but perfect, as if it was right there in the room with them.

"This is called a photograph," said Sisal. "A Glory invention. Focus, please."

Cora looked again and realised the picture showed a hospital bed, and a patient. The patient was Lilith. She was bandaged across her arm and head, and ribs, and one leg, and her eyes were closed. Her face was sunken and sallow. Automatically, Cora tried to *look* for the cause, but her head was too cloudy and she couldn't make anything out.

"What have you done to her?" she whispered. Her mouth moved properly, but her voice trembled and she clamped her jaw hard.

"Nothing," said Sisal. "She was injured while resisting arrest, and is receiving treatment." She watched Cora. "This photograph is from two days ago. I believe your powers extend one day? We assumed two, to be safe."

She nodded. "Lilith's injuries are severe and she needs treatment. And she will get it … *if* you cooperate. I don't know her location. The photographs will always be two days old before I get them – too old for you to use your tricks on them."

Cora stared again at the picture. It was so realistic she wanted to reach into it.

"It's all about planning, you see," said Sisal. "With proper planning, even the greatest threat can be contained. From what I've heard, you might be the most dangerous person in Colony!" She chuckled. "Why, you could kill me right now, couldn't you? Change the past, reach into my head, trigger a blood clot and *poof* –" she clicked her fingers "– I would be gone!"

She leaned forward. "*But so would Lilith.*"

She stood and smoothed out her skirt. "Get some rest," she said. "I just wanted to make sure you understood the situation before you tried anything rash."

Cora's head was still foggy, and she thought she might be sick. She clutched at the photograph until the paper ripped.

"Let us go, *please*," she begged. "I'm not a threat. What do you *want* from us?"

Sisal raised an eyebrow as if surprised. "Cora, I want your *help*."

She turned away.

"Wait!" Cora launched herself at the woman, but her legs were still numb and she collapsed and sprawled on to the floor. Sisal looked down at her, her black polished high-heeled shoes centimetres from Cora's face.

"Goodnight, Cora. We'll talk in the morning."

She glanced up at a point in the wall and nodded, and the door slid open. She left, and the door slid shut. A few seconds later the lights went out.

Cora lay on the floor and gradually pieced her surroundings together.

The door had opened on the woman's nod. Was it an electronic signal? Could she duplicate it? But no – when she *looked*, Cora saw a guard standing behind the door, peering through a tiny eyehole in the wall and lifting a heavy bar out of the way when Sisal nodded. Cora couldn't change the guard's orders, and she certainly couldn't move the bar. And everything in the cell had been set up more than a day ago – when she *looked*, the causes of their events were too old to see.

Perhaps when Sisal returned, Cora could rush past her when the door was open. But she suspected the woman had been telling the truth. She had no idea where Lilith was, and neither did the guard. She might be in this building, or a different one, or in Sheen, or anywhere. All Cora knew was that Lilith had been alive two days ago.

Cora's head ached. She dragged herself back to the bunk and gazed into the dark, trying to trace the water coming into the toilet cistern, and the air through the tiny vent, trying to find *anything*. Finally, she slept.

The lights came on a few hours later. Cora's internal clock told her it was seven in the morning. She felt better, clearer in the head. She peed and drank about a litre of water straight from the tap, and wondered what would happen next.

As if in answer, the door opened and Sisal entered, carrying a tray and a folder under one arm. The door closed and Cora heard the bar sliding back into place.

"Good morning, Cora."

Cora said nothing. The woman offered her the tray. "Breakfast. Go on, eat."

The tray contained a bowl of muesli, an apple and a cup of hot chocolate. Cora's stomach churned; she couldn't imagine eating. But Lilith would tell her to build her strength, so she forced the food down.

As she ate, Sisal watched her.

"You're a myth, you know," she said. "A wild tale of a girl turned into a *god*. When Perea's assistant Reeve came to us about you, all those years ago, we couldn't quite believe. The things he claimed you could do…"

Sisal shrugged. "We sent someone to retrieve you, but Lilith stole you away. And Reeve never could get the device working again. He died trying, and we gave up. Just another crazy Reverent story."

She smiled to herself. "But I never quite forgot about you. I've spent my career thinking about threats – threats to Colony, to Governor Thorsen, even to myself. But it was … *exhilarating* to think of all the ways in which you could destroy us."

"I don't want to destroy anything," muttered Cora.

Sisal pursed her lips. "Perea does though, doesn't he? I bet he'd like you to turn it all back and start again." Cora didn't answer, and the woman nodded.

"Well, I don't. You see, Cora, I am the Protector. It's my job to keep Colony safe. I don't want to undo it, I want to *help* it. And I want you to help it too."

Sisal handed Cora the folder. It contained another picture of Lilith. Perhaps the injuries were less severe in this picture, Cora couldn't tell. Just like the last one, the picture had been taken too long ago for her to use her powers.

"This was taken two days ago," said Sisal. "You can have a picture every day you cooperate. You'll be able to watch her getting better."

There was a sheet of paper in the folder as well, a printed report of a crime. In a box near the top it read "GLORY TECHNOLOGY THEFT, DOCKS".

"And this is something I would like your help with." said Sisal. "A crime committed last night – someone knocked out a guard and stole some highly dangerous Glory weapons. Citizens could die. I would like you to tell me everything you know about it."

Cora shook her head. "I don't know anything."

Sisal smiled. "But you could … couldn't you?"

Cora met her gaze.

She'd already *looked*, as soon as she'd picked up the sheet. The report had been placed on Sisal's desk by an assistant on the night shift, who had received it from a Protection Officer returning from the docks. In her mind's eye Cora saw every detail of the robbery, too – a blow to the guard's head with a short cosh, two men lifting boxes and taking them away…

She said, "I don't know anything."

Sisal looked down.

"These men are criminals," she said. "They stole weapons, and they will either use them or sell them. It's your duty to protect Colony. Will you help, or not?"

Cora chewed at the inside of her cheek. Sisal was right,

they *were* criminals. The man who had hit the guard didn't know if he'd killed him and didn't care. What would Lilith do?

She set her mouth firm. "I don't know anything," she said again. "Sorry."

Sisal considered her. She looked regretful, but not surprised.

"Well, that is your choice." She walked over to Cora, who flinched, but all Sisal did was collect the breakfast tray. She looked towards the wall; the door opened and she left.

Cora's heart thudded. She took slow breaths to calm herself, and closed her eyes in preparation for what would happen next. But nothing happened. The lights stayed on; Sisal didn't return. Cora waited, and wondered what to do.

Hours passed. She grew hungry. She spent the day examining every centimetre of the wall, trying to find any threads of cause and effect, anything to latch on to. The robbery was something, so she explored it as far as she could. But the men were horrible, and the more she *looked*, the less certain she was of her decision.

Sisal returned that evening with a tray of dinner. Another guard entered behind her, carrying a second tray and some bottles of water, and a few small vials of clear liquid. He put them down and left without glancing at Cora.

"Here," said Sisal, handing Cora the first tray. It held a bowl of tomato soup. Cora was ravenous and devoured it, picking up the bowl to drain the last few drops.

"You can have this one too," said Sisal, handing her the second tray of soup, and Cora nodded and picked up the spoon. She took the first mouthful and glanced at the other things on the tray – the bottles of water, the vials. She stopped eating and examined them.

"What are these?"

Sisal sat in her chair against the far wall. "Medicine," she said. "And painkillers of some kind. Rather strong."

Cora frowned. "I don't need medicine."

Sisal shrugged. Cora put her spoon down carefully. Her hand was trembling.

"This is Lilith's," she muttered. "Lilith's medicine. Lilith's … painkillers."

"As I said, it was your choice."

"But she *needs* this!" Cora's skin crawled at what it meant. "She needs water! And medicine!" *Painkillers. Oh, Lilith.* "You can't do this!"

"I'm not doing it. *You* are."

Cora threw the tray across the room, bowl and water and vials and all; they crashed against the far wall just a half-metre from Sisal. Soup spattered around her, but the woman didn't flinch.

"I'll kill you!" screamed Cora, and leapt forward. But still Sisal didn't move. She gazed into Cora's eyes, calm and cold and controlled, and her message was clear: *Then you will kill her.*

Cora stopped, panting, her hands clenching and unclenching just a metre away, and gradually wrestled herself under control. She bowed her head.

"All right," she said. Her voice was hoarse. "I'll tell you."

Sisal smiled and stood up.

"Tell me next time," she said. The door opened, and she left.

Cora blinked. "What? No! She needs the medicine! The water! Sisal! No!"

The door closed.

Time

Cora spent the night in darkness, in her cell, staring at the wall.

She tried *looking* at the spattered soup and the medicine vials, trying to track them back to Lilith, but without success. It was just a tray from the kitchens; there was nothing to see. She tried shouting for Sisal, for the guard, for anyone, but no one came. She sat on her bunk with her hands around her knees and eventually faded into broken sleep.

When the lights blinked on again, she flinched and peered up to see Sisal standing at the doorway with a tray. Sisal examined Cora, then walked across and put the tray down. A smell of hot chocolate rose from it. She returned to her chair and sat.

"Eat," she said softly.

Cora ignored the food. "One was tall," she said. Her

voice felt rusted. "The one who hit the guard. Blonde hair. Green jacket with a skull on the back. The other is younger, maybe twenty. Shaven head. He has a tattoo on his cheek – three blue stars."

Sisal waited for Cora to finish, then nodded.

"Thank you," she said. "That will be enough, I think."

Cora closed her eyes. "Is Lilith all right?" she whispered.

Sisal shrugged. "I don't know. She was already injured, but she's very tough. She may have survived. We won't find out until the next photograph."

She stood. "Eat. Preserve your strength. Colony needs you. Lilith needs you."

She left.

It was two days before Sisal returned.

A guard brought Cora's food. No one spoke to her, or made eye contact. The dried soup stayed on the wall like an accusation. Cora sat staring at it, hardly moving.

When Sisal did return, she had a picture. "A photograph every time you cooperate," she said. "This is from two days ago."

Cora looked at it and gasped.

In the first picture, Lilith had been injured, but recovering. Now she had collapsed. The photograph showed her dry lips cracked and bleeding, her cheeks sunken. Her bandages hadn't been changed, and the one on her leg was bloodstained and coming loose.

Cora screwed her eyes shut and clenched her jaw until the urge to wail had passed. When she looked up, Sisal was examining her.

"That was one day," said Sisal. "One day without food, water, painkillers, medical treatment. One day without your cooperation."

She sighed. "This seems harsh, I know. But I will do whatever is needed to protect Colony. It's important that you understand. Do you understand now?"

Numbly, Cora nodded.

"Good." Sisal passed her a report. "Another raid," she said. "Last night, at a research facility. No one harmed, but medicines taken and … certain documents."

Cora *looked* and saw a small group, dressed in black and wearing masks, breaking through the fence and creeping in. It seemed well organised.

"All in black," she said. "I can't make out any distinguishing marks."

Sisal smiled. "No, not a description this time. No, I want this…" She leaned forward. "I want this to have *not happened*."

Cora shook her head. "I can't just change things," she muttered. "If I could, I wouldn't be here."

"Find a way."

"I'm tired. I don't know if I can, I don't know—"

"I suggest you try," said Sisal coolly, "or it will be unfortunate for Lilith."

Cora, defeated, read the report again, and *looked* at the intruders. What could she do? The fence had an alarm, but … disabled? Yes, one of the group had disabled it. In fact, the change was simple: in her mind, Cora pinched two tiny wires together and a bell started ringing, and the group scattered, empty-handed.

But the raid had happened hours ago, and the trail of new consequences spread wide. People hoping for stolen medical supplies didn't receive them. Guards chased, assistants now wrote different reports, Protection troops weren't summoned, and in back rooms across the city, others were no longer reading the documents. Changes rippled out over time and Cora's head ached as she corralled them into this new reality, and the face of the Lady Nostic shimmered in front of her eyes…

She *fixed* it.

There was a pause, and then Sisal gasped. "That was *extraordinary!*" she exclaimed. "I can *feel* it!" She laughed in delight. "I can see both versions!"

Cora slumped on the cot. Something felt stretched inside her head, as if she'd sprained a muscle. Her nose was bleeding again.

"Can *everyone* feel it?" asked Sisal. "Is it just us? Does it hurt? Why is your nose bleeding?" Then she shook herself. "I knew, and yet I couldn't quite believe… How far back can you go? How often can you do it?"

Cora didn't answer. The photograph of Lilith lay next to her. Sisal smiled.

"You're tired," she said, standing up. "You have been most cooperative today. Colony thanks you. Please – eat your breakfast. Someone will clear your things away later."

She left.

Helping Sisal was a terrible idea, Cora knew. Lilith would tell her to refuse. Kill Sisal, escape, kill the guards, break the door open. Leave Lilith behind.

But Cora couldn't do that. When the lights went off she lay again in the dark and prepared for the next day. Dried blood cracked against her lip and chin.

"Omelette today," said Sisal. "I hope you like mushrooms."

Cora ignored the breakfast and opened the folder that came with it. There was a picture of Lilith, looking a little better. Her face was less sunken and someone had changed her bandages. She was still unconscious.

When Cora looked up, Sisal nodded, and handed over

another file.

"It was you at the warehouse raid, wasn't it?" Sisal asked.

It was the sixth day. Sisal had visited each day, with a tray of food, a photograph and a file. Crimes in Base, crimes in Sheen or Recon. Sometimes wanting just to know who was involved, sometimes wanting a change.

Cora tried to *look* whenever she could. She followed Sisal's footsteps back down the corridor to her office, to try to find out something about her – anything – but Sisal was careful. So Cora *looked* at the guard in the room next door, at the trays of food. She found the kitchens and followed the staff from their workstations. Gradually she built a map of the building in her mind, but it was exhausting work.

"Cora."

Cora blinked and looked up into Sisal's face. "I said it was you at the warehouse raid," said Sisal. "Tampering with the power supplies."

Cora frowned. "We weren't tampering. We *found* them. All the cells." She remembered Kai's comments: *The power shortage is a trick!* "Thousands of them, with no trackers."

Sisal nodded. "Who were you with?"

Cora ignored her question. "You told everyone there weren't enough cells. Why?"

Sisal sat back. She seemed gently amused. "You tell me."

Cora thought. What could possibly be gained by *pretending* to be running out?

"People think they're scarce," she said slowly. "So they agreed to you adding trackers to them. And now... Now you can find anyone using them away from the towns."

"Not just anyone," said Sisal, and smiled.

Cora shook her head as she understood. "Me," she murmured. "It was to find *me*."

Sisal studied her. "As long as there was a chance you were out there, you were a threat," she said at last. "An extraordinary threat. But an opportunity as well. Understand me, Cora. I will do anything I have to. I *will* protect the people of Colony. If necessary, I will protect them from themselves."

She handed over today's file. "Here, a riot in Sheen. They broke into a granary. Tell me who and how."

Cora *looked*.

It was hard to pin the riot down to an exact cause. It was like a fire with a thousand matches. But at one point the protesters had broken into a grain compartment and distributed its contents to others. A guard had left the door unlocked and unwatched.

"A woman and a man," said Cora. "The man has

black hair and a beard; the woman is a guard. She … accidentally left the door unguarded."

She looked up. "I don't understand. There was plenty of food – why are they so desperate?"

"The people of Sheen chose to vote against our necessary austerity measures," said Sisal.

"You mean there isn't enough to eat?"

"I mean there *may not be* enough to eat, in the future, and we are reminding them."

Cora stared. "You mean you're *starving* them because they didn't vote the way you wanted," she snapped.

"It's for the good of Colony," said Sisal, unperturbed. "People must understand that they have a choice: they can choose to cooperate, or they can choose the consequences."

She stood and nodded. "The perpetrators will be dealt with," she said. "Colony thanks you."

She left. Cora stared at the photograph again until the lights went out.

Each day another photograph, another mission. Sometimes information – descriptions of demonstrators, where they had been, who they had met. Sometimes a change – have this alarm go off, have this person fail. Have this person be seen; have *this* person be *not* seen.

Cora searched every time for the least destructive paths, but she could see the effects mounting. Demonstrations were stifled, actions thwarted, peaceful protests broken. People kept their heads down and stayed out of trouble.

Steadily, Sisal was using Cora to tighten her grip around Colony.

"Everything you do is for the citizens, you know," Sisal said, one morning. "We are protecting them."

Cora ignored her. She sat, dead-eyed and limp, on the cot. Sisal frowned.

"You should eat. Lilith needs you to keep your strength up." She eyed the blood crusted below Cora's nose. "You're trying too hard."

Cora shrugged. "You're making me do it," she said in a dull voice.

But Sisal shook her head. "No. You're trying to escape, all day long, aren't you? You'll kill yourself at this rate. And then…" The woman leaned forward. "What would happen to Lilith?"

But Cora continued, mapping out the building from scraps of details. Her head pounded from her efforts, following people as they walked around and interacted in tiny ways. Every night she tried to see further back, but she couldn't, no matter how hard she strained and sweated. Her bones throbbed.

The endless *looking* bruised her. Her skin hurt and she felt dizzy when she stood up. Her nose was bleeding too much, and the Lady Nostic appeared to her day and night, with that look of calm concern on her face, saying words Cora couldn't hear.

She continued anyway. She imagined she was Lilith; indestructible, unstoppable. She persisted.

As Cora weakened, Lilith grew stronger. She was still strapped down, but her leg was mending and the bandages around her head had been removed. One photograph showed her awake and glaring at the camera, as if glaring at Cora herself. Cora suspected Sisal was deliberately slowing Lilith's recovery, but what could she do? How much was she prepared to do, to keep Lilith alive?

The answer came on the eighteenth day.

"Nothing serious today," said Sisal, handing Cora the file. "Just some young offenders causing trouble, but it's been going on for a while."

The folder held a blurry photograph of three teenagers running down a street. They wore masks, and Cora *looked* almost without thinking, searching back through cause and event until she found the room where they'd put the masks on. There, she could see it. Three teenagers—

—And one of them was Gavin.

Cora felt her heart thud. "I don't know," she said.

"Yes, you do. Don't try to lie. You know I'll find out."

"It's blurry. I can't always see."

Sisal leaned back. "Are you really going to do this to Lilith again?"

"Please," begged Cora. "Please, you must believe me, I'll do anything—"

"Then *tell me*," demanded Sisal. "Tell me what you know, or Lilith will face the consequences!"

Cora swallowed. She had to save Lilith! But Gavin... All the people she'd affected – she'd managed not to think about them as real, she realised. She'd managed to not think about the changes she was making. The lives she'd hurt. But this was Gavin. Gavin was real. They were *all* real. And she realised she couldn't do it any more. Not even for Lilith.

She closed her eyes. "No," she whispered.

Sisal nodded. "Very well."

She left. Cora slumped back into her cot. *Oh, Lilith, I'm sorry*.

She searched for an escape for the thousandth time, but there was nothing – her only contact with the world was the water in the cistern and the faint breath of the air vent. She closed her eyes and wept, and nearly missed it. That one moment...

The air flickered. Just a tiny hiccup, an echo rattling through the internal vents of the building and into her cell. Just a whisper.

Gunfire.

Saved

Gunfire!

So faint that Cora could hardly hear it, but unmistakable, and from somewhere in the complex. Almost without thinking, she *looked*...

The sound came from a gun, fired by a guard. The guard was firing at a group who were raiding the building. They were raiding the building because of a plan, made in a secret meeting. A boy talking to others about a threat...

It was Gavin.

"Gavin!" Cora jumped to her feet. And not just Gavin, she realised. Kai had been there too, and they'd been staring at a map of the building, and a room kept separate from the others, locked with a bar...

"Return to your bunk!"

Cora whirled, but there was no one there. The voice

had come from the other side of the wall, the guard. Cora *looked*. The guard had called out because he was nervous; nervous because he'd heard on his radio that there was a problem... The radio had picked up signals in the air. The signals came from a transmitter in the centre of the building. How easy it would be to simply cut the connections, disable the transmitter...

Cora *fixed* it, and reality changed. Now the guard had never received a signal, had no idea a raid was happening. Everywhere in the building, guards were trying and failing to get status updates, but their radios heard nothing. Cora grinned.

She felt a tiny tremor under her feet and *looked*... Someone had set off explosives in one corner of the building, a distraction designed to let a smaller group move further in. Cora stood in the middle of the room, waiting for anything, any slight effect she could decipher to tell her what was happening, and to help if she possibly could. A sound, a scent, a vibration in the walls...

A very faint bump from the guard's room. She *looked*. The bump had been caused by the guard putting a bar against the inside of his door, the one out to the corridor, because his radio had gone dead. Cora frowned. The bar was too heavy and solid for her to change, but the guard still had to walk over to the door, legs moving, nerve signals firing…

The bundle of nerves in his back was as delicate as a coin in flight; Cora imagined it, very briefly, *pinched*, and the guard collapsed as soon as he tried to stand up. "Sorry," she muttered, and *fixed* it. A few seconds later the inner door opened and two figures stood at the doorway, dressed in black and wearing masks, staring at her. One carried a gun. A third figure pushed past them and pulled off his mask.

It was Kai.

"Cora!" he shouted. He rushed towards her and hugged her.

The last time Cora had seen Kai, she'd screamed at him. He'd betrayed her and lied to her, pretended to be her friend. But she hugged him back as hard as she could, and hot heavy tears sprang into her eyes until she could hardly see.

"We're here to rescue you!" he said.

"I know!" laughed Cora through her tears. She looked up at the other two as they lifted their masks, revealing Gavin and a man she didn't recognise. "Gavin!"

Gavin nodded but didn't smile. The man pointed his gun at her. "Rescue," he growled. "Yeah. Or maybe just sort it out right now, yeah?"

"Stop it," muttered Gavin. "You know that wouldn't

work anyway."

Sort it out? What did he mean? Why wouldn't Gavin look at her?

Kai dragged her out. "Come on!" he shouted. "We've got to go!"

Outside her cell she saw the guard's room. The guard lay on the floor, and the man pointed his gun at him as they passed and seemed angry when Gavin pulled him away.

"We have to get to the lifts!" shouted Gavin.

"Have you got Lilith?" asked Cora.

Gavin stopped. "What?"

"Lilith, have you got her? Do you know where she is?"

"Lilith's *alive*?"

"We've got to go!" growled the man.

"Not without Lilith!"

The man swore. "No!" he snapped. "*This one's* the mission, we can't do both! We don't even know where she is!"

Kai said, "There was another protected area."

"Shut up!" said the man, but Cora was already *looking*. She saw Kai and Gavin and the others peering over the diagram of the complex, and there were *two* isolated rooms: hers … and a hospital bay.

"That's it!" she exclaimed. "It's down here, come on!"

She ran, and a second later she heard them chasing after her. Kai caught up with her.

"Do you know what you're doing?" he asked. He looked terrified.

"Yes!" she said. "We can save her!"

They raced down a flight of stairs and along two more corridors. Gavin moved to the front, with the angry man at the rear. Kai shepherded Cora, who was trying to *look* as she ran, searching for any consequence and preparing to *fix* it. A guard came round the corner and fired, but Cora made his gun jam. She staggered, clutching her head.

"Which way?" called Gavin.

"Left!" They barrelled through a set of doors into a small medical area. It seemed deserted. "Far door!" said Cora. "Lilith! Lilith!"

Gavin ran towards the door, but it was already opening.

Lilith stood in the doorway.

She was gaunt, her skin bleached and grey under the harsh lights, and she wore a hospital gown that made her legs seem spindly. In one hand she carried the broken side-rail of a hospital bed, still chained to her wrist, and in the other she held a syringe as if it were a knife.

She nodded to Gavin. "Nice of you to show up," she said. "Does your mum know you're out?" She looked up and saw Cora, and her face changed to a look of, a look of…

Her leg buckled beneath her and she collapsed.

"Lilith!" Cora raced to her. "Lilith, are you all right?"

"Yes! Yes, I'm OK. Good to see you. My leg's dodgy. Let me get up. Come on." But Cora wouldn't let go, and after a moment Lilith put her arms around Cora and hugged her, hard.

"Hey," she whispered. "It's OK, Cora. It's OK."

"I couldn't get to you!" wailed Cora, pressed against her. "I couldn't get to you, and I couldn't get out!"

"I know, I know."

"And they made me change things, they said you were dying, oh…"

"It's all right now, love," Lilith murmured. "Everything's going to be fine."

"We've got to go," said Gavin. "They'll be locking the place down; they'll know where we are."

Lilith nodded. "Give me a hand up."

Gavin and the man leaned down and hoisted her to her feet. She put an arm around Gavin's shoulders.

"There's a service elevator at the back," she said. "I heard the nurses using it."

They headed towards the back of the ward, but they

261

couldn't move quickly. Lilith could barely walk, and Gavin and Cora had to take almost her whole weight. They came around a corner and saw the elevator at the far end of the corridor, but then there was a shout, and the sound of footsteps behind them, running hard.

"Guards!" shouted the man. He swung back round the corner and fired four or five times. The running stopped, but a barrage of gunfire returned as he retreated again. Gavin checked the corridor to the elevator and scowled. He and Lilith looked at each other.

"Damn," muttered Lilith.

Cora didn't understand at first. Then she looked down the corridor and realised. It was too long – they wouldn't be able to reach the elevator before the guards came round the corner, and once they did, the corridor would become a deathtrap. They could hold here, but nowhere else.

She heard more guards running towards them – too many for her to use her powers. Soon there would be someone with a smoke bomb, something that could go around corners. They couldn't run and they couldn't stay.

They were trapped.

"What do we do?" she asked. Could she stop their bullets? One, perhaps two. Not hundreds.

"Well, we know how this ends," said Lilith. "Better get

on with it, eh?" The angry man glanced at her, hesitated and nodded. "I miss my crossbow," she muttered. "Just for the look of the thing."

Gavin handed his over without a word. Lilith nodded. "Good. Gun?"

The man gave her his.

"OK." She nodded. "Cora, come here." Cora came up and Lilith hugged her again, a solid, hard hug, arms wrapped around her tight as if she was trying to transfer something important.

"You did well," she whispered. "But you mustn't ever use your powers like that again. Not ever. Understand?"

Cora nodded.

"I'm so proud of you," said Lilith.

Cora held her tight. "I had to save you," she said.

"I know, and you did, Cora. You saved me." Lilith smiled. "You saved me your whole life. Now I'm saving you."

"What?" Cora felt a sting; when she looked down, she saw the syringe. "What?"

Her knees buckled immediately and Lilith's face splashed into a blur. Gavin caught her as she slumped. She blinked, trying to wash away the tears in her eyes.

"What did you do that for?" Her mouth moved awkwardly. "What?" She tried to *look* back, to *fix* it, but she couldn't focus on anything.

"Keep her under for at least thirty-six hours," said Lilith. "Otherwise she'll undo it." Gavin nodded, and he and Kai took a shoulder each and dragged Cora to the elevator, with the man following. Cora's head seemed too loosely attached. She tried to see where Lilith was, and then looked back.

Lilith wasn't with them. She was still at the corner, holding the gun in one hand and the crossbow in the other, looking calm and relaxed.

"Lilith?" Still Cora's mouth wouldn't work properly. "Lilith?" It was too hard to focus. The edges of her vision were closing in under a grey sparkly nothing.

"Lilith!"

Lilith watched from the end of the corridor as they dragged Cora away, and just for a moment her face seemed completely different; it had an expression of soft longing, a crooked smile of regret, and pride, and love…

Then she held up her gun in salute and grinned.

"Come on then!" she roared. "*COME AND GET ME*!"

And she stepped around the corner, shooting as she went.

"*LILITH*!"

They ran to the elevator and crammed in. Cora stretched her arms back towards Lilith but she was nearly unconscious; she could no longer lift her head. The last thing she heard was the sound of heavy gunfire behind them as the door closed.

Then everything was gone.

Glory Day

Cora lay half awake for a long time, in a formless state where shapes came and went as shadows and blurred patches of light. Voices washed over her like water. She thought only of the expression on Lilith's face in that last moment. Her look of goodbye.

After what felt like a thousand years, she started to focus. The patch of light was a window. The shapes were people, moving back and forth. Her arm hurt. People were talking around her.

"Is she safe? I mean, are we *sure* she's safe? Maybe we should dose her again."

"No more drugs. Let her wake up, for goodness' sake."

A familiar face loomed over her. Lilith? No. No, of course not. The face smiled. "Welcome back, child."

Juliet.

"How long?" Cora tried to ask, but her throat was too

dry. She knew the answer anyway, automatically; two days, nearly.

Juliet said, "You're safe here. They can't find you."

Oh, Lilith! Tears welled up in Cora's eyes but she couldn't move her hands to wipe them. Juliet dabbed them away with a handkerchief.

"Sit me up," she croaked. Juliet gently lifted her and propped a pillow behind her head. A wave of nausea swept over her and she closed her eyes until it passed, then looked around. They were in a room she didn't recognise, with yellowing plaster on the walls and a few broken pieces of furniture, and a tiny kitchen.

Juliet and Lotty were by her bed. Gavin stood a few metres away, watching her carefully.

"This is a safe house," said Juliet. She smiled, but her eyes were red. "They raided our place."

"How are you feeling?" asked Gavin. His voice was cold.

"Weak," said Cora. She tried to concentrate. "Thank you for rescuing me."

He shrugged. "Didn't have much choice."

"Be nice," warned Juliet.

Gavin scowled as if biting down on his words. "Kai worked it out," he said. "We thought you'd left town with Lilith, but then stuff started happening. People getting arrested, anonymous tips. Things … changing. We could *feel* them change sometimes." He looked away. "Kai worked it out."

"I had no choice," Cora whispered. "They were going to kill her."

Gavin shrugged. "She would have told you to let them."

"I know. I couldn't."

"You should have."

"Leave her alone!" snapped Juliet. "Would you have let *me* die? You'd kill your own mother?"

Gavin hesitated, and then ducked his head.

"Where's Kai?" Cora asked.

"Around," said Juliet, patting Cora's hand. "He sat with you yesterday; he's getting some rest."

"He's a liar," whispered Cora. "You can't trust him."

Juliet frowned. "He said you'd had a fight," she said. "He said it was his fault. He was devastated. And this rescue… He persuaded the groups, you know. He's the reason you're here."

Cora shrugged. "And Lilith's dead."

Juliet bowed her head. After a moment she reached into a pocket and slipped something into Cora's hand. "I found this when we were leaving the house," she said. "I thought you might want it."

It was short, heavy; sharp at one end. A crossbow bolt.

Cora closed her fingers around it.

"She wasn't really my mother," she said at last. There was a feeling like a cloud of liquid black smoke in her chest. It pressed down on her, making it hard to breathe.

"Of course she was, child," said Juliet.

"I mean, not my real mother."

But Juliet shook her head and wrapped Cora's hand in hers, around the crossbow bolt. "Yes, she *was*. In every way that matters, even when she didn't know it."

Cora said bleakly, "She said she could feel it when I made changes. Any change, not just ones that affected her. That's how she found me. How could that be?"

Juliet smiled sadly. "Because everything you did affected her. Because you were her daughter."

I'm so proud of you, she'd said.

"Oh, Juliet, I'm so sorry," Cora sobbed suddenly. "I tried to save her but I wasn't strong enough, I couldn't get her out, I didn't know what to do and Sisal had these pictures, *photographs*, and, and—"

"Hush, love, it's all right—"

"No it's *not*, she made me do it and Lilith's gone, she's *dead*, oh, Lilith, oh, Seleen, oh…" She fell into tears and the black cloud crushed her, and the tears didn't let it out; it stayed within, sick and solid, and there was nothing she could do, and Juliet's arms were around her now and

Lotty was holding her hand and she cried, cried forever, and she felt Juliet's tears mingling with hers on her face, until eventually she sank back into sleep.

She awoke an hour later to the sound of laughter coming from outside – laughter, and singing, and a noise of crowds. Torchlight flickered at the windows.

Juliet and Lotty were asleep on a sofa. Gavin was still there. Kai was there too now, watching her.

"Hey," he said softly. His blue spiked hair had collapsed into a mush and there were circles under his eyes. His usual smile seemed long gone. Cora gazed at him without speaking.

"Good," said Gavin. "I'll tell the gangs you're awake."

"Gavin, I'm sorry," said Cora. "I couldn't—"

He waved a hand in a half-dismissive, half-angry gesture. "Whatever." Then he sighed. "It's OK," he said in a slightly softer voice. "I know."

"She's not ready to talk to the gangs," said Kai. "Let her be, come on."

But Gavin shook his head. "That was the deal."

"What deal?" asked Cora.

Gavin shrugged. "Me and Kai, we persuaded the street gangs, set this all up. Took a while for them to believe us, but you're our *superweapon*. Everything you've been doing against us – now it can be *for* us. With your power, we can *fight* them now! Fight Sisal! Fight Thorsen! Smash it all down!"

Cora's head ached. "Smash it all down," she repeated.

Gavin grinned. "Yeah! So we can rebuild!"

"Can't rebuild with dust," she murmured.

Gavin frowned. "Look, I think you're still a bit fuzzy with the drugs. But you're *amazing*, Cora. Sisal and Thorsen must be wetting themselves right now. With you on our side, we'll be unstoppable!" He turned to Kai. "I'll be right back, OK?" Kai nodded, and Gavin left.

Cora sat back in the bed and closed her eyes. Her head felt a little better. Her body felt hollow, as if the black cloud had gone. It hadn't, though. It had melded with her, settled like dark liquid in her bones and bloodstream. She thought about Lilith.

Cora hadn't saved her. All her powers, and so many people damaged because of her. So easily controlled and manipulated. Chased and captured, rescued, drugged. Used. And Lilith still gone.

She sat up.

"Hey, what are you doing?" said Kai. Cora ignored him. She sat on the end of the bed and waited for the nausea to pass, holding the crossbow bolt tight in her fist.

"Seriously, you should take it easy—"

271

Cora glared at him, and he stopped. "Why did you bring me?" she asked. "To Perea?"

Kai ducked his head and looked away. "He raised me," he mumbled. "At the orphanage. He's a good person, and he asked—"

"Take me to him."

"I don't think that's a good idea."

Cora stood up. She wasn't sure if she could, but she managed. Her feet were lumps of pins and needles, and she stumbled forward, and Kai had to catch her. At his touch, she stiffened. Dull pain flared in her head. She remembered Lilith hugging her so tight, as if trying to share some vital piece of herself. A sliver of Lilith, in her head. Saying…

Get moving, girl.

Cora ground her teeth and took a step, and Kai had no choice but to walk with her.

"Take me to Perea," she said again, and heard Lilith's voice.

Kai bit his lip. All his bravado seemed to have burned away, and he looked very young suddenly. He nodded. "OK. Wait, hang on." He fetched a coat and wrapped it around her, and led her to the door. Cora glanced at Juliet and Lotty, still asleep.

Keep going, said Lilith's voice.

They opened the door and the street was full of people shouting and cheering, singing and laughing. Cora flinched and tottered back. "What…"

"It's just the party," said Kai. "It's Glory Day."

Crowds were walking along the street, laughing and chatting, following banners and wagons. Some were dressed in strange outfits, some were carrying flaming torches, some were juggling or spinning objects up into the air. Cora and Kai joined and let the river of people sweep them along.

"Keep your head down," muttered Kai, and Cora saw Protection troops lining the edges of the parade. They seemed to be only interested in the celebrations, but she kept her head low as they passed. Within her, the black smoke roiled and the crowd's laughter sounded like the cawing of cruel birds.

The parade led into the main square, and Kai and Cora peeled away towards the Sanctuary building. Its front was lit up for the celebrations, but around the back it was full of shadows and they crept in silence.

"Hey!"

A guard stepped out of the gloom. "What are you doing around here?" he asked. "This is a protected area."

Cora ignored him and kept walking.

"Hey!" The guard moved forward, but she stared at

him and suddenly his eyes closed and he slumped into a faint. Beside her, Kai shivered.

"Did you do that?" he muttered.

"Move," said Cora.

They crept into the Sanctuary building, entered a dimly lit passageway and stopped outside the ornate door to Curator Perea's office, still damaged from where Lilith had kicked it in. Cora entered. Perea was at his desk, writing; when he looked up, he didn't seem to recognise her at first. Then his face shone and he stood.

"Cora!" he said in a voice full of joy. He saw Kai. "You found her! You saved her!" Then he frowned. "My child, what has happened?"

Cora shrugged. "Lilith is dead."

The old man's face fell. "I'm so sorry. She was an extraordinary woman."

"She died because I wasn't strong enough," said Cora. She swayed, almost fell, but she dug the little metal bolt into her palm and focused. Kai held her arm. "You can make me strong enough to save her."

"Ah." Perea studied her, and then looked away for a moment. He seemed to be debating with himself.

"Child, you cannot save her," he said at last.

"I can," said Cora. "If you make me strong I can."

"I mean," he said gently, "you cannot *save* her. I can

complete the process, but she cannot be saved. None of us can."

He lifted his arms. "Look at us. We're the last floating survivors of a shipwreck. This isn't living, it's clinging to the wreckage until we slip away and drown. What would saving Lilith's life do? These lives are *meaningless*."

Cora shook her head. "I don't…" She fell silent.

"Lilith lived around death and destruction, and her existence was nothing but loss. And we are *all* like that – all of us! Lilith, me, you, Kai. This isn't how the world was meant to be. This isn't what you were *created* for."

Cora peered at him. He seemed very far away, and the edges of her vision were grey.

"I can complete the Uplift," he said. "But don't save us. Save the *Glories*. Do you understand? Undo *all* of this. Prevent the Fall!"

She couldn't stand up much longer. Her body was collapsing and eventually willpower would not be enough. It hadn't been enough for Lilith. Lilith was dead. Sisal, crushing the people she was supposed to serve. Kai's parents, her own parents. Anish. Lives broken and distorted until they were not lives at all. Black smoke.

Cora nodded. "Yes."

"Cora, are you sure?" asked Kai. He seemed suddenly uncertain.

"Yes," she said again, and shrugged. "Yes, why not."

Perea sighed a trembling breath. "*Yes*."

He led them through the corridors of Sanctuary, to the room containing the Uplift bed. He reached around his neck and removed a chain. On the end of the chain was a small flat box with a star carved on the front, and inside was a sliver of green plastic, covered in fine strands of gold. He inserted it into a slot in the base of the bed and a panel lit up, showing the outline of a human body, a green blinking light, and a single word.

The word was *Consequences*.

"What do I do?" asked Cora.

"Just lie here," said Perea. His voice shook. "The machine will complete the Uplift."

Cora lay down. The padding crackled as she lay on it, and it smelled of old dust. The sides of the bed came up around her like a coffin, and the metal arm loomed above her head. Kai and Perea gazed down at her.

"There is a word they had," Perea said in a quavery voice, "though they did not think it applied to them. The word is *apotheosis*. It means to be transformed into a god."

He shook his head and reached for the controls. "You know what you must do," he whispered.

"Yes."

"If this works ... none of us will ever have existed."

Cora nodded.

"*Good*."

Perea started the machine.

Apotheosis

The metal arm of the Uplift device swung over Cora and she flinched. But it didn't touch her. Instead it peered at her with two small green lights, like eyes. They pointed to the top of her head and swept down to her feet, then back. The lights became brighter, and Cora felt a strange prickling at the back of her head.

"Analysing," said a voice, and she almost jumped. It sounded like it came from inside her head. Kai and Perea didn't seem to have heard it.

"Where are you?" asked Cora.

Perea looked down in surprise. "I'm here, my child," he said.

Cora shook her head.

The voice spoke again. "Standard Uplift process has been initialised but not completed. An additional module, *Consequences*, was initialised but not completed. Complete

Uplift and module?"

"Yes," said Cora.

The light paused.

"There are security warnings associated with the *Consequences* module. Contacting server... Server unavailable. No information available. Continue?"

Cora blinked at the lights. What did that mean?

"Um... Yes?"

"Completing Uplift. Please lie still."

The lights flickered, and she felt a sensation like heat, an itch like a thick hard scab that she wanted to dig and scrape away. Her hands twitched but she stayed still. The mechanical arm moved up and down her body, sometimes widening to bathe her in light, sometimes narrowing, before returning to her head and focusing the light to a point inside her that made her want to scratch and scratch and never stop.

The light blinked out and the arm moved to the side and stopped.

"Uplift complete," said the voice.

Cora lay on the bed and gazed up at Kai and Perea's worried faces.

"Are you all right?" Perea asked. Cora considered. She felt a little light-headed, and ... different. She felt a background *hum*, as if only now noticing something that had always been there.

"I think so," she muttered. "Wait."

She examined Perea's long, crooked nose. How had that happened? she wondered, and *looked*…

And an explosion of images appeared in front of her, vivid and glowing and stretching further back than she could ever have imagined. She was watching a ball game in the Sanctuary courtyard on a cold January sixty years ago: a young man was holding the ball and running towards a post, but he was pulled down by another and his face crashed against the ground.

The boy had the ball because the player in front of him had passed it at the last moment, seeing the incoming tackle. Which was caused by a thousand moments in the game that brought the player to this position, and Cora saw them all, precise and clear and beautiful. She saw everything leading up to it. *Everything*.

She watched the boy's nose crack against the cobbles and imagined it differently – the fall at a very slightly changed angle, moving his head to the left instead of the right so the nose did not break. She saw the consequences stretching out – no blood on the stones, no dismay, no sigh every time the young man looked in the mirror for years, a different face now beaming down on her. She held it all, this new reality, she could *fix* it…

Cora took a deep breath and exhaled slowly.

"Yes," she murmured. "It worked."

Dust hung in the air, tiny particles that speckled as they turned. Turned…

She saw the dust, caught in faint air currents like a twig in a river. She saw the air currents, caused by the three people in the room. She saw their movements, and every event and counter-event that had led to this one moment, this single dancing dot of ancient dried skin – she could see all of history, in a speck of *dust*.

"Warning," said the Lady Nostic.

Her familiar face appeared to Cora, ghost-like and pale. But this time Cora could hear her. And she knew instinctively what to do; she focused, and the woman's image sharpened and filled out. Now she was in front of Cora as if she were real, standing in a white room, and then Cora was *in* the room with her, and Kai and Perea were gone.

Cora gasped.

The room was large and circular. Smooth pale walls curved about them, and the ceiling arched high above her head. In the middle hung a huge, moving sculpture. It started and ended at two points several metres apart, and between the points floated a cloud of shimmering gold, made up of millions of tiny pieces. The pieces were flat, and showed pictures too small for Cora to make out. They fluttered like trapped birds, tethered to each other with almost invisible threads.

"Hello," said the Lady Nostic.

She was as beautiful as ever. Her skin was smooth and perfect, her hair was black silk, cut short. Her green eyes seemed to smile like her mouth, and her teeth were even and white. She stood with her hands clasped lightly in front of her.

"I–I can hear you," said Cora, and then felt embarrassed. But the Lady Nostic just smiled.

"Welcome." She bowed slightly. "I am the Diagnostic System."

Cora gazed at her. "You're the Lady Nostic."

The woman cocked her head. "I am the Diagnostic System. But you may call me Nostic, if you like."

"Who *are* you?" Cora's voice felt strange as she spoke, as if her mouth wasn't really moving. But the woman seemed to hear her.

"I am the Diagnostic System. I monitor for errors and warnings associated with your Uplift."

Cora looked around at the white room. "Where are we?"

"We have not moved. This is an image projected on to

your cerebral cortex by pseudo-neural software written into modified non-replicating DNA in the parietal region of your brain."

Cora blinked. "I don't know what any of that means."

"I can adjust my vocabulary. Please wait." The woman's image flickered. "I am a special kind of machine known as *software* inside your head," she said at last. "I can make your brain see and hear me as if I were standing in front of you."

"So you're not real?"

"I am real software, but I am not physical. I am the Diagnostic System. I have been activated because there are warnings associated with the Uplift module you are using. The module is named *Consequences*. Warning: There are security issues with this module. The *Consequences* module has unexpected side effects."

Cora frowned. "What's wrong with it?"

"The *Consequences* module allows users to see the timeline of events leading to particular situations. However, it is more powerful than intended. It appears that *Consequences* can also be used to modify temporally pre-occurring events."

Cora tried to understand. "You mean … changing the past?"

"Correct. There are security and health implications.

This module should not be used."

Cora examined the cloud again and walked towards it. Then she stopped and looked down at her feet, confused.

"How can I walk?"

"I am creating the illusion of walking and talking, corresponding to signals from your cerebrum."

Cora nodded. Magic.

Up close, each golden ticket appeared to be a tiny scene. Some of them seemed familiar. "What is this?" she asked.

"This is your Causality," said the Lady Nostic.

It was hard to know how many tickets floated in the cloud. The more Cora looked, the more there were, all interconnected. She examined one near the end and realised that it wasn't really an image; it was more like … like…

Josif sits at the desk in his guard room, checking on the prisoner. He's worried because his radio has stopped working. His orders are to bar the outer door if anything like this happens, so he walks towards it, but feels a sharp sensation in the small of his back and suddenly his legs go numb, and he collapses to the ground with a grunt of surprise.

Cora gasped in shock.

"That was me!" she said. "In the cell, during the rescue. *I* did that."

The little golden ticket was attached to others, and she recognised the ones ahead. A girl running down a corridor. A woman standing in an infirmary, with a broken bed rail in one hand and a syringe in the other. And behind were more images, events that had led to these scenes. And somehow she knew that if she looked now, the cloud would be different – there would be a ticket for every event that had led to *those* events…

"This is your Causality," said the Lady Nostic again. "It is the continuum of every event and decision that brought you to this moment."

The golden pieces spread out from a single event at the far end, formed the cloud, and then narrowed back down to a point near her, which seemed to froth as new images bubbled up, like water from a spring. The last one was her talking to the Lady Nostic now, while lying on the bed in Sanctuary.

Cora searched back to where she had been, and a little further ahead. She found a hospital ward…

A small group of desperate intruders are in the corridor of a hospital ward, pinned down under enemy fire. A woman in a white gown makes a decision, hugs the girl she has never called daughter and prepares to save her. The others drag the girl away and the woman checks her weapons. She gazes back one last time, smiles at something she finally understands, and then turns and walks into a storm of gunfire.

Cora watched the scene, though it stabbed at her; watched every bullet that hit Lilith, every finger on every trigger and every decision from every guard. And she knew she could change it all now – stop the guns from firing, change their paths, she could *fix* it…

Child, you cannot save her, Perea had said.

Cora peered at the tickets, casting back through Lilith's history. Years on a mountainside, damaged and brooding. Hiding – not just from hunters, but from the loss of a man she had loved more than she thought possible. And further back, to a street in Base, thirteen years before…

Two bodyguards, the best in Base, step cautiously out into a street. Behind them are a man and a woman, holding a tiny baby girl. The woman has straight black hair and pale, golden skin like Cora's; the man is blond and bearded. One of the bodyguards is Lilith, looking astonishingly young, and Cora realises the other must be Anish. Anish seems serious but not grim, his eyes are kind, and his hair is curled and beautiful. The street looks clear, but someone has betrayed them, and as they leave the building they are ambushed. The man and woman are killed. Lilith is shot, but Anish throws himself in front of her and saves her life. As he falls to the ground, dying, his face has the same smile Lilith's will show, many years later.

Cora watched, and watched, and watched. Her parents died. Anish fell. Cora was stolen, to be re-stolen by Lilith.

Tears ran down her cheeks and black smoke swirled inside her.

Child, you cannot save her. Because Lilith's life was already broken; broken for thirteen years. And if Cora went further back? To the people who sent the killers? To the world they lived in, died in? Was any of it worth saving?

Save the Glories!

Cora considered the cloud, and walked towards the far end, where all the events came together into one point.

Her head hurt. It was somehow hard to walk to the end, even though it seemed only a few metres away, like wading through a fast-running river. She pushed on. Back, before any buildings existed except those left by the Glories. She reached for a ticket and found herself looking at the very first survivors of the Fall…

They awoke on a bitter winter's day with no memory of what happened, or even who they were, and no way to work the technology around them – many died in the first winter and now the rest huddle in the shelter of these old walls, seeking sanctuary. It is a dark age, full of hunger and violence. But they hold on to flickers of hope – myths of Glory days, when there was food, and warmth, and the faint memory of a woman who protected them, a woman they call the Lady Nostic.

Each step was harder than the one before it, even though Cora knew there were no steps, just illusions. Still, she felt the pressure against her, and a dull pain in her head. Back to a morning…

A man wakes up with a confused grunt. There is something wrong, but he can't work it out at first. He realises — slowly, and then with panic — that he cannot remember his name, or where he is — he cannot remember anything.

Now Cora stood at the far end of the cloud, at the point where there was one, single event. She reached towards it.

"Danger," said the Lady Nostic, and Cora jumped. "Danger. This action is dangerous to yourself and others."

"I need to see," said Cora. "There's been a disaster; the Glories are gone. I need to fix it."

"This action is dangerous to yourself and others."

The Lady Nostic's voice was calm, but she was staring at Cora. Cora found it hard to meet her gaze.

"Sorry," she muttered. "I have to do this."

With one more heave, she reached up and grasped the very first ticket, the event from the exact moment when the Glories had Fallen. It trembled in her hand as she stared into it. She frowned.

"I don't understand—"

Everything vanished.

There is nothing.

There is a maelstrom of nothing. Time collapses with space and churns like a cauldron of boiling water in front of her, around her, and she is a speck, a vanishing point, a moment blasted aside. Frantically she tries to pull back, but there is nowhere to go back to, nothing to show her how to return.

Cora screams, but no one hears her. There is no one to hear. There are no Glories. There is no Colony. There is nothing but chaos.

The world is gone.

Outcomes

Kai stared down at Cora and knew something was terribly wrong.

"It worked," she'd said, after the metal arm of the Uplift bed had stopped moving. But then her gaze had lost its focus, as if she was seeing something they couldn't. Her lips had moved but she had made no sound. Who was she talking to? Now she lay completely still, her breathing steady, her face calm. She seemed like she was asleep. But her eyes flicked to and fro under her eyelids in panicked bursts, endlessly, as if searching for something, or caught in a nightmare.

"Something's wrong," he said.

Beside him, Curator Perea shook his head. "Nothing is wrong, Kai. She completed the Uplift! Did you not feel it?"

Kai shook his head. "I felt something." He had – for a

moment the world had seemed to shudder around him. "I don't know. Was that it?"

Perea nodded. "She has become a *Glory*. And she is doing what only a Glory could do. Remaking the world! Bringing them back! Undoing *everything*!"

Kai looked up into Perea's watery eyes. The old man was trembling, his whole body shivering in excitement. "That's…" He hesitated. That was what they'd planned, wasn't it? When Perea had prepared him for his mission, sent him to Sheen and Recon to search for Cora. *Bring the Glories back*, he'd said, and Kai had agreed. And now everything they had strived for was happening, just as they'd hoped.

Kai gazed at Cora, so thin and vulnerable and bruised. He knew he should feel joyous. But what he thought instead was: *this is my fault*.

Another ripple shuddered through them both, and the walls, and the bed. Cora's eyes darted this way and that. Kai's instincts screamed.

"This is wrong," he said.

"What?"

"There's something wrong. She's in danger. This is *wrong*!"

He leaned towards Cora and put his hand on her shoulder. She didn't move. He shook her. "Cora? Cora, can you hear me?"

She wasn't breathing.

"Cora, wake up!"

Cora was in chaos.

She hung above, below, surrounded by the roiling, noiseless nothing, pinned and helpless. There was no sense, no logic, just heaving static that churned and spat and stretched out towards her. She tried to pull back, but she couldn't tell which way back was. She tried to *undo*, with all her strength; power ripped from her in shockwaves but had no effect.

The Lady Nostic's face appeared. "Danger," she said.

"Help!" screamed Cora.

"Danger. You must disengage you mussssst dis-dis—"

"What *is* this?"

"Possibility event horizon collapse multiple temporal recursive-recursive-recursive—" The Lady Nostic disappeared and Cora was alone.

She couldn't disengage. She didn't know what disengage meant, she didn't know which direction she was coming from or to, and the wave rose under her, the sky fell in on her, the whirlpool sucked her towards it—

"*Cora?*"

She reeled. "Kai?"

"*Cora, can you hear me?*"

"Kai, is that you? Where are you??"

"*Cora, wake up!*"

Where was he? Cora concentrated – *there*, a direction she couldn't even describe. But she pointed herself towards him, imagined his voice was a rope and dragged herself along it. She was on the edge of something she couldn't see or touch or understand, and one side was insanity and the other was unreachable. Her heart lurched, but she pulled again, *heaved*—

And she was back in the white room.

Her lungs burned and she dragged a ragged breath, coughed and tried again. "What was that?" she gasped. "What *was* that?"

"There was a system malfunction," said the Lady Nostic.

Cora groaned. "I don't understand what that means."

"No stable reality exists beyond this point. Causality is fractured."

"But… How?"

"*Consequences*," said Lady Nostic. "The *Consequences* module was installed by all users. When its unexpected abilities were discovered, users attempted to modify temporal causality simultaneously. There was a system malfunction."

Cora's breathing slowed. She looked at the woman. "You mean … everyone used it?"

"Correct."

"And they *all* tried to change the past? All at the same time?"

"Correct."

That was what she'd seen. Waves of events and consequences, everyone trying to change reality, over and over, competing and destroying. Everyone trying to rewrite the world, everyone trying to make it magically better, to be *their* version of better. All at once…

Cora realised her hand was over her mouth in horror. "How did they stop it?"

"A group of users realised what was happening. They worked together to create a single, shared reality where all the Uplift software failed. The system became stable again, but all users were affected. Their internal software crashed."

"But I don't understand," said Cora. "Why would the *Glories* want to change things? They were perfect!"

"They were not."

"But they were the Glories!"

"They were human."

The gold cloud shimmered in the silent room, spreading out from the single moment of the Fall, people waking up with no working memories, no idea what to do or how to survive.

Cora shook her head.

"But then I can't fix it," she said. "I can't change *that*."

We are clinging to wreckage, Perea had told her. *Save the Glories!* But there was nothing to save. The Glories had destroyed themselves and there was nothing Cora could do to stop it. And all the suffering since that moment… She felt the black weight again in her chest. She felt helpless, like she had inside the chaos.

"I thought I heard Kai's voice," she said.

"Kai is currently in the room with you," said the Lady Nostic. "Would you like to hear him?"

Cora nodded and Kai's voice echoed around the room.

"*Cora*," it said. "*Cora, wake up!*"

"*Leave her!*" said Perea's voice. "*She is saving us!*"

"*I don't want her to save us! I want her to wake up!*"

Cora bit her lip. Kai had lied to her, then risked his life to rescue her; betrayed her and then saved her. He was here.

"Can I talk to him? Can I show him … this?"

"Kai does not have the modifications needed to fully immerse," said the Lady Nostic. "However, prosthetic devices are available. Please wait."

"She can't hear you, boy," said Perea.

"She *can*," insisted Kai. "She heard me. She's breathing again. Cora!" Tears pricked his eyes. "Cora, this isn't right," he muttered. "Come back, please. I made a mistake. I'm your friend. I'm sorry. *Please*."

The base of the bed clicked.

Kai looked down. Where the side had been smooth, there was now a thin rectangle. It slid open with a hiss of air to reveal a tray containing a pair of gloves and something like goggles.

Kai picked up the gloves. They were dark grey, made from a slightly clammy material, with thin wires running up inside them. They seemed to change shape to fit his hands.

"She *can* hear me," he said. He put on the goggles. The glass was clear. Two small pellets hung to the sides, and after a moment he realised they were to go into his ears. It felt ridiculous; he almost laughed.

"I don't know what I'm supposed to—"

The room vanished.

In its place was a large, gleaming-white area that curved away behind him. Kai yelped and grabbed the side of the bed. He could feel it but no longer see it; when he looked down, his hands seemed to be clutching at empty space.

Carefully, he let go with one hand and waved it in front

of his face. He could see his hand moving. He tapped his chest and felt it.

"It's fake," he muttered.

"What?" asked Perea's voice, strangely muted.

"I can see a room. A fake room, like I'm in a painting, and…" Kai looked up. Ahead of him there was a huge, fluttering cloud of gold. In front of the cloud stood a tall woman whose face seemed familiar, and next to her was Cora.

"Hey," she said.

Kai swallowed. "Hey," he managed.

Cora gestured towards the woman. "Kai, meet the Lady Nostic."

"Oh!" Kai gasped, and tapped his forehead with his hand. She smiled at him.

"Hello," she said. "I am the Diagnostic System."

Kai gawped at her, then at Cora. She was smiling too, but seemed brittle. "Where are we?" he asked. "What is this?"

"It's like a pretend world, in my head," said Cora. "We're still *out there*, but we can see *here*."

"Um … OK." He nodded to the cloud behind Cora. "What's that?"

She shrugged. "Everything."

Kai didn't know what to do with that answer. As he

looked at the cloud, he found himself drifting towards it.

"I'm moving!" he said, alarmed.

The Lady Nostic – *Oh Glory, I'm talking to the Lady Nostic!* – smiled again. "You are using a prosthetic interface system to interact with this shared virtual space," she said. "You can focus on any area to investigate."

Kai kept moving until he was close enough to see the cloud. It was made of millions of golden tickets, each one a tiny picture.

"It's called the Causality," said Cora. "It's everything that's happened, to anybody."

She waved towards a single point at the far end, where all the tickets seemed to start.

"That's the Fall. It was the Glories. They did it. They broke everything."

Kai frowned. "I don't understand."

Cora shrugged again. "It doesn't matter. Look at it. This is everything that happened – to me, to you, everything stretching back."

She grimaced.

"And it's all *death*."

Kai started at the venom in Cora's voice. She sounded as if she was trying not to cry.

"I can't stop the Fall," she said. "I tried, but it's too *big*. And the Glories did it. They did it all, they caused it, it

298

was *all their fault*. I can't stop it. I can't save them."

She sniffed. "I could save Lilith. I mean, I could save her life; it would be easy. But I've seen what would happen – she'd never forgive me, not again. And I can't *really* save her. I can't make her be not broken."

She turned away from him, towards the cloud.

Kai said, "Cora, I'm sorry. You saved my life, you trusted me, I'm really sorry, I never meant—"

"It doesn't matter." She didn't look at him. "You're just broken too."

She reached into the cloud, plucked a ticket out and showed it to Kai. It was a scene from inside a cabin in the woods. Thin trails like cobwebs linked it to other tickets before and after.

"There's us, see?" she said. "There's you lying to me." He winced.

She reached for another. "And here's me, now. I'm here because Lilith died. She spent thirteen years crushed by losing Anish. He died because a man named Whorley betrayed them. Whorley was blackmailed by Sisal into stealing me. And all because Curator Perea was obsessed with restoring the Glories. And back, and back."

She let go of the tickets and they settled back into the cloud. She shook her head. "Stupid decisions. Bad luck. Selfish, greedy people. Crushing us all, ruining *everything*."

There was something fractured in Cora's voice. Kai felt as if he was stretched out over a frozen pond, listening for the crack of ice.

"Cora, you're not well."

She sniffed. "But I realised, while I was waiting for you. I realised I can fix them."

Go to her, he thought. *Hug her or something.* But he was too cowardly.

"What do you mean?" He shook his head. "I thought you said you couldn't save them."

"No," she agreed. "Not the Glories, or any of us; we're too broken. But some of the ones after." She walked to a point close to the start. "Here, look."

She showed Kai another ticket, a picture of a woman. He stared into it and saw…

It is a month since the Fall. It has been a terrible, nightmare time, but this woman is smart and tough, and she leads a group of survivors to safety. She understands that they must work together to survive, and to preserve their humanity. Together, with her guidance, they have a chance. But the icy rocks are treacherous; she slips and cracks her head, and dies.

"Whoa!" Kai gasped. "What was that?"

"It's what happened," said Cora. "This woman died. The group fell apart, they fought; some of them were killed, some starved, some died of cold."

300

She waved towards the cloud. "That's what this all is," she said. "People failing; people dying. Good people suffering; bad ones winning. But I can save her. I can't save the Glories, but I can save her. Watch." She did something to the ticket; it flickered, and the whole cloud rippled into a new shape.

Kai stared. "What just happened?"

"I made her survive," said Cora. "She doesn't slip on the ice. She leads the group for decades and everyone's happier."

Kai looked at the new tickets, twisting, everything different. "You changed all of *history*? Glories' blood…" He frowned. "Wait – how come we're still here? Wouldn't we be changed?"

Cora nodded. "Oh, yes. Once I *fix* it into place, we'll all be gone. You, me … Lilith." She shrugged. "It doesn't matter though. These people, *they're* the new civilisation. No dark times, no hunger, no cold. They'll be happy. I just need to protect them, and make them be good."

And she smiled.

It was her eyes, Kai thought. They didn't focus properly; they glossed over everything without landing. Was it this illusion of a world? Were his like that?

"Is there something wrong with my eyes?" he blurted, and felt foolish.

Cora looked at his face for a split second, and away. "No." She moved further ahead. "I can make the world right," she said. "I can replace us all with a *better* version.

"Watch."

Consequences

Cora held a ticket, and the ticket was death.

It showed a group of raiders. Kai realised it was a scene from a few years after the Fall, in the new reality that Cora was creating…

The lands beyond Base are full of raiders. Desperate and cruel, they've hunted the wildlife until there is nothing left, and now they march towards Base. They are wary – the people of Base are strong. Led by a shrewd, determined woman, its people work together and share what they have. Time and time again the raiders have attacked, only to be beaten back. But the woman is old now, and her son is weak and foolish. This time when the raiders throw themselves at the walls, the son panics. He runs, leaving his post undefended, and the raiders burst through – and conquer the city.

"There," said Cora.

Kai watched in horror as the raiders destroyed the settlement.

"That's *awful*," he muttered.

Cora shrugged. "Yes. But I can fix it." She moved her hand across the ticket, and it changed. "There."

Now Kai saw…

The son runs, leaving his post undefended. The lead raider leaps at the wall, but slips on a patch of ice, collapsing before he can reach the top. The man behind is too close and staggers into him, and they tumble in confusion. It's a tiny delay, but long enough for the settlers to get a crucial defender in place, and the defence holds!

"You saved them!" said Kai as the cloud rippled forward. But Cora frowned, and looked ahead to another scene…

The raid is defeated, but now that the danger has passed the son claims credit for their victory. With the support of a few of his cronies, he deposes his mother and seizes control. He is a selfish, cowardly leader, and he undoes the work his mother achieved – dividing the group, weakening them, taking for himself, leaving them ruined and starving.

"Stupid, greedy, *coward*," Cora hissed. "You see? Good people create things and bad ones tear them down. Do you see? Do you?"

"Yes," said Kai sadly.

Cora smiled a cold, hard smile. "But not any more." She reached out again, back to the previous ticket – and now…

304

As the raiders loom into sight, the son panics. But before he can run, he suddenly grips at his heart and collapses to the snowy ground. Another man steps forward to lead the defenders and the gate holds – the settlement is saved! The old woman mourns her son but part of her is relieved, for she knew he would be a bad leader. The man who held the gate becomes her second-in-command, and together they lead the group well.

Cora nodded. "There."

Kai gazed at the cloud in its new shape. His mouth was open, he realised. It was better, of course. The group survived, they were happier, but…

"Did you…" He hesitated. "Did you just *kill* that man?"

Cora looked at him, her strange eyes glinting, and shrugged. "He would have died anyway."

"Well, yes, but—"

"But *nothing*. He would have died anyway, and this way we save the settlement. He was a bad person. We don't want bad people in our world."

She smiled another odd, glassy smile. "Look."

She pointed. Everything was different. The settlement was a shining point of civilisation. Raiders who gave up their violent ways were welcomed, given food and shelter. It was a place of hope.

"You see?" she said. "It's for the good of Colony."

Cora moved along the cloud, reaching into it again and

305

again. She pulled moments out, changed them, showed Kai; prevented accidents, corrected decisions.

"*This* man," she said. "Not this woman, *this* woman. Save him. Let——" She paused. "Let her die," she muttered.

Kai watched as she rebuilt the world. It was only fifty years since the Fall but the people of Colony were thriving. Happy, healthy, lucky – oh, so lucky! They worked together, sharing and helping and building a future. They remembered the lessons of their first leader, but it was more than that. They didn't talk about it, but everyone knew: in Base, good things happened to those who were good, and bad things to those who weren't.

"They're doing it themselves now, you see?" said Cora in satisfaction. "They understand, they *have* to be good."

"I guess," said Kai. "But…" *But what?* He couldn't say. There was something. "But they're scared," he said at last.

She looked at him. "No they're not. They're happy."

"Only if they do what you want."

"I want what's best for them."

"But they don't have any *choice*."

Cora stopped. "What?"

"Well, you know…" She gazed at him with her blank eyes, and Kai's words dried up.

"They have a choice," she said, in a strange, hard voice.

"Like Lilith – she chose to die. That was *her* choice. She chose to leave me. *That was her choice.* People make *bad* choices, Kai, and bad things happen to them – but I can *stop* them."

"Or cause them? Like to that man?"

"He doesn't *matter!*"

Kai gasped. Cora blinked. "I mean, because he was going to die anyway."

"We're *all* going to die eventually. You're taking away their choices—"

"They have a choice!" she spat suddenly. Her face turned dark and her hands clenched. Power seemed to come off her in waves. "They *have* a choice! They can choose to *cooperate* or they can choose the *consequences!*"

"You can't do this, Cora!" he tried. "You can't just bend people into what you want!"

"What I want?" she demanded. "What I *want?* What I want is for Lilith to be *not dead*, don't you understand? *And she won't let me change that!*"

It was too hard to look at her. It was like staring into a black sun.

"Cora—"

"She lied to me, Kai! And she *left* me! So here I am fixing everyone, but not her, because she didn't *want* me to! I'll make them all be happy and she'll still be *dead!*"

307

She was panting, as if struggling to breathe.

Kai said, "But you can't be a *god*!"

And Cora laughed.

"Why not? Why not, Kai? Look at me – I'm a *good* god. I'm taking all this and making it *better*. It could be worse, you know. It could be so much worse. It could be the way I feel inside, *all the time*."

"Cora—"

She stepped towards Kai suddenly, and he recoiled.

"You want to know how bad it could be?"

"No, all I'm saying—"

"How bad the world *could* be, if I wanted it?"

"No, please—"

"*Look!*"

She reached up, grabbed a point in the cloud and dragged it into a new, darker shape.

"THERE!" she screamed.

The raiders recover, find another gap in the wall and storm the settlement. They burn and destroy everything, tearing down the helpless survivors, burning their world.

"Cora!"

"Shut up!" She swept events across the Causality. "THERE!"

With the mysterious Glory weapons they steal from Base, the raiders storm across Colony, attacking and taking and crushing.

Never uniting, they fight each other to the death, raise tyrants, destroy lives. Black fire devours the world.

"THAT'S WHAT IT COULD BE!"

"Stop it, Cora, please!"

"AND THERE! AND THERE!"

Every moment of hope is gone. The world is despair and cruelty, and a lurking spectre that crushes anyone who tries to make things better. Survivors huddle against walls, whimpering, waiting to die, seeing others only as threats to be feared or victims to be robbed and killed.

Kai gasped. The cloud was a black, roiling mass, every image one of failure and loss.

"ARE YOU HAPPY NOW, SELEEN?" Cora screamed. "YOU'RE DEAD, THEY'RE DEAD, IS THAT IT?"

"Cora, *please*—"

"*IS THAT WHAT YOU WANTED?*"

She swayed, panting, glaring at the dark web. The room was silent. Kai stared in horror at the images shimmering in front of them, twisting slowly as if in a faint breeze.

Gradually, Cora's breath steadied.

"There," she muttered in a thick voice. "That's what it feels like."

She gazed at the ruin for a few seconds. Then she sighed, as if breathing out black smoke, waved a hand,

and the cloud reset. It rippled back until everything was as it had been. Her head drooped.

Kai moved towards her and placed a hand on her shoulder, carefully, as if she might catch fire under him. She shuddered, but didn't move away.

"I'm sorry," he said. The words were useless, but they were all he had. "I'm so sorry."

She sniffed.

"She always knew," she murmured at last. Her voice was dull and flat. "That's why she wouldn't let me save her. She was trying to save *me*; save me from ever using my powers. She understood, you see?" She stared at Kai, and through him. "She knew I would never be able to stop."

She watched the cloud and the little tickets flickering and turning, and folded her arms over her chest as if in pain. "This power. It wants me to be a god. Sisal, Perea, even Gavin, they want me to be a *god*. What do I do?"

"I don't know," said Kai.

They stood in silence, and the cloud shimmered.

"I made a mistake," Kai said at last. "Curator Perea told me we could restore the Glories and I agreed, and I found you and brought you here. And now Lilith is dead, and it's because of me.

"I'd give anything to undo that. Anything. But then

what? You could undo Anish's death, make it never happen. But you only know Lilith *because* he died. All the moments you had with her came from that. Every selfless thing she did. Would you undo that? This…" He waved at the cloud. "You can't change their past. That's what people *are*."

"Then what's the point of any of it?" muttered Cora. "What's the point of people if they die and *leave* you?"

Kai moved his lips but couldn't speak. He couldn't think of anything. At last he said, "Maybe we can make things better. Some people do."

Cora raised her head. Her face was pale; there were no tears in this illusion world, but Kai thought she was crying. Her eyes were bleak, but at least they no longer had that dreadful, glassy sheen.

"Juliet told me something once," she said. "I remember, she said…" She walked towards a point near the end of the cloud, searching, and plucked a ticket out and showed it to Kai. "Here."

It was an image of a woman.

A woman sits at a sewing machine in a tiny house in Base. Next door, her daughter is completing her homework, because the woman insists, demands, that her children grow up smarter than her, wiser than her, better prepared to move the world forward. She doesn't always succeed, but she tries, and she makes their home a warm bright circle of hope and love. Now she sits at the machine, fixing a patch on to a damaged leather jacket. Her son wanted to throw it away, but she is fixing it, because the only way to make the world better is to take the broken things you have and try to mend them.

They watched her together.

"I know what to do," Cora whispered at last. She told him.

Kai nodded. "Are you sure?"

"I think so. Will she … forgive me?"

He smiled. "It's all she ever wanted for you."

It was a tiny change, but the effects spread wide. Cora watched them scatter out, small at first, slow, but then exploding into action and consequence, people drawn in and affected, and affecting others. Ten thousand tiny impacts spread over a lifetime, a hundred thousand, more. She watched them flutter out into the Causality, then gathered every thread of her new reality together until she held them all, every one…

And *fixed* them.

Actions

When Cora awoke, it was as if from a very deep sleep. Her bones felt heavy and relaxed, utterly comfortable, and gradually she became aware of the edge of the blanket on her face, and thin sunlight against her eyelids, and the smell of heather and lavender and pine. She opened her eyes and gazed up at the ceiling of their little cabin, back on the mountainside.

She stretched and sat up.

The cabin was empty. Cora looked around, thinking back to the night of the attack – soldiers bursting in, front and back, stun grenades and chaos. She saw the rough table and chairs, and the countertop, and herbs hanging from hooks in the beams. She smiled.

The door opened and Lilith entered, wearing her leather trousers and hunting jacket, and carrying a rabbit. She placed the rabbit on the counter and stopped, facing away. Then she nodded and turned to face Cora.

Her face moved between a scowl and something else. She said, "I didn't know if you were going to wake up." Her voice sounded rusty.

Cora nodded. She felt a flood of golden light within her at the sight of Lilith, a joy that made her bones sing. "How long was I asleep?" she asked.

"A day." Lilith sniffed. "I'll make some tea."

She turned back to the counter and put a kettle on to the stove. Her shoulders seemed stiff and she moved awkwardly. She spent a long time spooning tea into the pot, without looking at Cora.

Cora watched her happily. She realised she could still feel the world where Lilith was gone. The grief was still there, the black smoke in her mind, the despair. She understood it, and it would always be there. But it had merged with this gold, into something deeper. Bad things had happened, could happen again, but she was stronger now. The joy and grief combined had become her strength.

"How much do you remember?" she asked.

Lilith paused. "Everything, I think," she said. "I remember both … versions."

Cora nodded. "Some of the others who were affected will remember too, little bits. Like a dream. But you see everything, because it affects you most." *Because everything I do affects you*, she thought.

Lilith turned and leaned against the counter with her arms folded. "What did you change?"

Cora remembered the moment, in the storm of chaos and possibilities, where she had decided. The course she'd chosen, out of everything she could have done to transform the world.

"I broke the Uplift machine," she said at last. "I made it fail, when they first ran it on me. When I was a baby."

Such a tiny change, in the end. All it needed was a tweak to the processor, too subtle to even see, but enough to ensure it would always fail and revert to safety mode, and the machine would complete but with no effect.

"So I never had any special abilities. Ever."

"But Sisal still tried to steal you," said Lilith, frowning. "I don't understand – that's why we're *here*, because she tried to steal you."

"She didn't know it had failed then," said Cora. "It took Perea a while to go through the readings and work it out. Then his assistant, Reeve, told Sisal, and she lost interest."

Lilith nodded. She gazed out of the back window.

"You made yourself ordinary," she said at last.

"In a way."

"And all this time we've been hiding, no one's been hunting us."

"No," said Cora, smiling. "Nobody cares."

Lilith looked as if she was about to say something, but the kettle boiled, and she shook her head and poured the tea.

Gavin blinks as he stands around with his friends, realising he's been staring into space. The others haven't noticed; they're talking again about Protection troops, and Sisal, and how they have to get rid of them all. Gavin nods, though he wonders how this will happen. What they need, he thinks, is someone like his Auntie Lily, the one his mum is always going on about. She could make a difference. After a bit, he makes his excuses and heads home. Lotty's cooking tonight, he thinks. A bit of home time would be nice.

Kai feels an extraordinary sensation of double-ness as he runs, a sense that he has run this way before, or has never run this way, or is running in two different worlds at the same time. It is so disconcerting that he almost loses his balance, and the stallkeeper lunges for his collar.

But the boy recovers and skids around the corner and away from the marketplace, and the keeper, cursing, returns to his stall to see what has been stolen. A couple of apples, he thinks. Stupid kid.

Kai stops to catch his breath and gives one of the apples to a thin-

boned child staring at him from the other side of the road. He winks to the child and heads back up to Sanctuary, biting into the other apple, crunching the fresh fruit, wondering what the day will bring.

While in a large, wood-panelled room in Sanctuary, Curator Perea tries to focus on a report from one of the masters, about an orphan under Sanctuary's care. The master despairs of the young man and his antics, but Perea has always had a soft spot for the lad. Perhaps he could be a Seeker, he thinks. He has good instincts. Perea longs to investigate the Glory "beds" scattered around Base, all broken now, of course. They'd found a live one once, but it hadn't worked, and things had ended badly. Still, there was always hope. Smiling, Perea takes a sheet of paper and writes a tactful reply, offering to help.

And across Colony, people awake from dreams or moments of déjà vu, seeing a different world. Old Jeb Harrow has a nightmare that Seleen's cabin was on fire. Juliet stares into her sewing machine, unseeing. And somewhere in Base a short, neatly dressed woman sits at a desk covered in reports and realises that she has been daydreaming, a wishful fantasy about a girl who could see and change the past, who could undermine her enemies, help her control Colony, and keep it safe…

Cora drank her tea and inhaled the steam, hot and sweet. She looked up to see Lilith staring at her again. She smiled, and Lilith shook her head.

"And that's all you changed?" Lilith asked.

"Yes."

"Why?"

Cora put down her mug. "You mean, why didn't I do more?"

"Yes."

"Take down Thorsen? Kill Sisal? Save my parents?"

"Yes."

"And Anish?"

Lilith bowed her head. "Yes."

Cora sighed. "Because you were right. I could have been a *god*. I could feel it. I had the power to change people whenever I wanted, into whatever I thought was better for them. And that would have been terrible.

"If I'd stayed as I was… It's too hard to resist. Someone like Sisal would have tried to force me to do it. Gavin would have asked me. I would have wanted to. But we can't change the past; it's everything that created us. The things that happened to us, the decisions we made, the things we regret, the way we cope when things go wrong – that's who we *are*. We can only change the now. Mend the broken things, even if those broken things are us. Try to be a bit better than we were."

She shrugged. "We can't remake the past. We have to

fix the future."

Lilith said, "But Thorsen's still in charge. And Sisal."

"Yes," said Cora. "But we can't just wish them away. I saw what happened to the Glories, Lilith. They had this power and it destroyed them. It nearly destroyed me. We have to do it the hard way. You stood in the corridor to save me. That was your decision. And I saw Anish, defending us." Lilith looked up. "He sacrificed his life for you. He was magnificent."

Lilith said nothing and bowed her head again. After a while she scrubbed her hand over her face and stood.

"Got to sort out the animals," she said in a gruff voice.

Cora sat on her bunk and watched the steam rise gently from her tea. She took a long breath, held it for a moment and let it go. Then she stood up.

When Lilith returned, Cora was out of bed and already dressed, packing clothes into a canvas bag.

"What are you doing?" Lilith asked. "You should take it easy. You've had a hard time." She looked at the bag. "Are you going somewhere?"

"Base," said Cora. "If we get to Recon today, we could catch the transport tomorrow morning."

"Why do we need to get to Base?"

Cora shrugged. "We've got to help. Gavin's there, and

Kai. Curator Perea too. They need us."

"I don't understand," said Lilith, frowning. "Help with what? You want to start an uprising?"

"No, I want to stop one." Cora smiled and pulled her bag closed. "It's still a democracy, you know. Thorsen and Sisal are in charge because we put them there. People get the leaders they choose, and that's how it has to be. We have to persuade them to choose better ones."

She felt different as she talked. She realised she'd grown taller without noticing, with a confidence that reminded her of someone else. She no longer felt like something hidden away, or cargo passed around. She felt, suddenly, like someone who made her own decisions. She felt as if she *shone*.

"But it's corrupt," said Lilith. "It's hopelessly corrupt; you can't win."

Cora nodded. "I'll need people who know their way around corrupt systems, like Kai."

"And the population just does what they tell them. There's no interest in change."

"Perea can be our contact with the Reverents. He can help us get people motivated again. And Gavin knows about the government's secrets; we can expose them."

"But you don't have your power any more!"

And Cora laughed.

"I *have* power, Lilith! Don't you understand? We *all* do. I have the same power as everyone else – I just have to *use* it. We all have to use it, every one of us. *That's* how we make the world better. That's how we fix things."

For once, Lilith seemed to be lost for words.

"It's dangerous," she said at last.

Cora stopped. "Yes. I'll need a bodyguard. Someone I can trust."

She stood in the cabin, caught in winter sunshine that glowed against her hair, tall, young, unafraid. She reached for the jar of dried beans, took one, and held it out.

"I'll hire you," she said. "If you'll take the job."

Lilith gazed at her for a long time. Then she gave a wry smile, took the bean, and nodded.

"I guess I'll get packing then."

They ate a small lunch of bread and cheese. They didn't talk much. Occasionally Lilith looked up at Cora as if to say something, but stared out of the window instead. It was a cold day, but bright, and the sunlight lit up motes of dust in the cabin. Cora savoured the rough texture of the bread and the creamy smooth cheese. She watched the dust drifting in the air, and smiled.

Then Lilith packed her bag and they left.

"I'll get Jeb Harrow to look after the animals," she said,

closing the door. "You reckon we're coming back?"

"I don't think so."

Lilith nodded. "He can have the whole cabin then." She looked up at it. "I liked this place." She sounded wistful, and a little surprised.

"So did I," said Cora. "But it's time to come down off the mountain."

They headed down through the woods and towards the pass.

"So what's your plan?" asked Lilith. She walked fast, in her usual long-legged gait, and Cora matched her stride for stride.

"Head to Recon," said Cora. "Take the transport to Base. Find Kai and the others. After that…"

She grinned.

"We're going to fix the future."

Acknowledgements

This book is about what happens when everything has gone wrong.

Sometimes it can feel like we're living in that world right now, right? Scary events in the news can make us feel like we don't have any control. Weird politicians are making weird decisions and telling us that we agreed to them. Old prejudices and intolerances have raised their horrible heads, when we thought we'd got past all that nonsense. It can all seem a bit ... doomy.

So I am lucky to be surrounded by people who make the world a little better. At Nosy Crow there have been Tom, Hester, Rebecca, Sîan, Hannah, Alice and so many others keeping things going – thank you! Dan Mumford keeps creating glorious book covers that make me drool. Thanks to my agent Caroline Montgomery of Rupert Crew Ltd, and my friends at Visible Ink for support and virtual biscuits. Here's to all the librarians, teachers, classroom assistants and volunteers who've kept sharing the love of reading and storytelling despite everything, you legends. Thank you to Scottish Book Trust for tireless support, and to all the bookshops – you're all just lovely :-) Hello Fiona and Matthew at Blackwell's Edinburgh!

Above all, I am lucky with my family. Mum and Dad showed me, through their incredible efforts, how love and humour could face down disaster. Now my own daughters are blazing into the world and explaining things to me I never understood. And to Catherine … I don't even know where to begin (though maybe with *Law and Order* reruns and chocolate gingers).

The quote at the start of this book comes from Thomas Paine, who saw that there was a better way to live – a way to change a system that seemed fixed in place forever. "We have it in our power to begin the world over again," he said. Not by magic, or superpowers, but by believing that we can make a difference. We *all* have power; we just have to use it. We can't change the past…

But we can fix the future.

Alastair,

Edinburgh, 2022